Tortured Innocence

© 2017 Shantel Brunton

Hey Petra

You are super awesome. You're sweet and
funny, and I hope you love the book

- Shantel Brunton

TORTURED INNOCENCE

Chapter One

It was my sixth birthday, and everything was falling into place. I looked proudly into the mirror. My silky blonde hair fell just a little bit past my shoulders. It wouldn't be like that for long, though. Since it was my special day, Daddy said that I could get it styled just the way that I wanted it. I knew exactly what I was going to do; I was going to have that hairdresser shave it right down to one itty bitty centimetre just like Daddy's. After I got my hair cut, I would look so much more like him.

We shared many similar features: the same blonde hair, large hazel eyes, and naturally tanned skin. But he was so fierce and intimidating—very tall, muscular, and fit. His voice sent chills down your back. Not me, though. I was his Nikki, his precious little Nicole.

Mom always called me Nicole. She wasn't like Daddy and me. She stuck out like a neon blue line on the sands of Afghanistan, with her pasty pale skin, long frizzy black hair, and blue eyes. I was her mint bud just the same.

"Ready to get your army fuzz, Nikki?" my dad called to me.

"Oh yes, sir." I gave him a salute and bowed like he was a king.

"You're relieved of duty, soldier."

"Yes, sir."

He laughed a laugh that shook the room with great thunder and picked me up as if I were no heavier than a feather. Then he bounced me up in the air and held me securely. "You're no heavier than my weights."

I snuggled against his face. His prickly whiskers rubbed roughly against my cheek. All the while I breathed in the musky scent of his aftershave. "I love you." I sighed happily.

"I love you too, Nikki. Now come on. Let's get you your cut. You're going to look so beautiful and mature. But you want to know something?"

"What?"

"Mama's going to cry when she sees you."

I leaned over and whispered in his ear softly. "Well, why don't we make sure to save her an extra special lock of hair?"

He chuckled and carried me off to the truck. I was well fastened in and quite enjoying myself. The rides with him always went so fast. In no time, we were at the barber shop. It had a big spinny pole on top of it; the pole had white and blue stripes swirling round and round. I loved that pole!

When we got inside Daddy lifted me out, carried me into the shop and plopped me down in one of those big black chairs. Turning to the barber, he said, "We want this shaved right down into a crewcut."

I couldn't help myself; I started squealing. "Yes, army fuzz, army fuzzy." Daddy motioned for me to settle down, but his smile still did not fade.

The lady gasped. "Does she really want that? Are you sure?" I giggled. She looked like a clown. Her red hair was all frizzy; she was wearing too much red lipstick that had smeared on her upper lip, and clumps of white eye shadow stuck around her eyes. "Her hair is so healthy. Why do you want to wreck it?"

My father's eyes clouded. "She'll look beautiful as always."

Clown Lady shook her head, but she started shaving anyway. Clumps of hair fell down my back, on my shoulders. Some strands even rested on my eyelids and eyelashes.

My already short hair was reduced to centimetres in just a matter of minutes. The lady looked angry at my father, but I didn't care. I took a few seconds to stare at my new reflection. My hair was in short fuzz or, as Dad called it, a crewcut. My tanned skin that was no longer hidden by hair seemed to highlight my hazel eyes even more. Dad pulled out two crumpled twenty dollar bills before Clown Lady even had to ask. She accepted them as if they were bombs that would blow her head off.

"You can keep the change," he said politely. He shook her hand, and she winced. He did have quite a bone crushing grip that nearly broke your hand.

I looked down, noticing a longish strand of hair resting on my shoulder. I plucked it up. "We should save this one for Mom."

"She'll cry, for sure," he laughed, and with that, he scooped me up, my strand of hair tucked softly in my hand. The ride home was short but comfortable. My mother greeted us at the door. Her long hair was pinned up neatly, and she wore a pleasant smile.

"Well, I was wrong; your father was right. You do look like a beautiful princess!"

I giggled and handed her the lock of hair. She gasped and playfully punched Dad. "I told you I didn't want any hair." She squatted down and stared intently at me. "You know I have a black lacy silk ribbon tucked up in my jewellery box. You go tie it in a bow the best you can, and I'll keep it safe forever."

"Promise?" I asked expectantly.

She nodded "Cross my heart, and if I lie, I shall die."

I was content with the answer, and so happily I sprinted up to their room and did as I had been asked. I could hear my parents talking downstairs. Their voices soon grew hushed and worried. I hurried down as fast as I could, thinking there was something seriously wrong. My mother was crying, and my father was holding her hand. His cell phone lay discarded on the table.

"What's wrong?" I cried helplessly. It took them a few moments to answer. In those awful moments I stared at their blank, absent faces.

"Honey, your dad is going back to Afghanistan to train soldiers for six months," my mother responded choking on sobs. He put his hand on hers and squeezed gently. This was a big deal. He had gone to Afghanistan many years ago, and when he returned he still had a job in the military training soldiers. But that was here in safety, not in Afghanistan where there were bombs and terrorists.

"I'm going to be fine," he whispered to her. "I'm not in a war zone. I'll be where the land is safe."

I clapped even though a few tears welled in my eyes and a painful lump was forming in my throat. "You'll do great, Daddy." He gathered me in a warm embrace and sat me in the middle of the couch; I enjoyed being in the middle very much.

"Mint bud, you're so brave." Mom paused and then gently ran her hand over my fuzzy head; I felt nice and peaceful.

"Well, let's get some popcorn and watch a movie," Dad suggested. The remainder of the night rolled by pleasantly. My parents popped the popcorn and poured extra melted butter on it. We all had our choice of drinks too. Dad had Coke; Mom had an orange crush, and I had an all-natural ginger ale with real ginger.

We had all curled up under a thick warm comforter, and by ten o'clock I had fallen asleep. Daddy had carried me up to my room. I was in my pyjamas and being tucked in, when I woke up.

"Daddy!"

"Hey, soldier."

"Where's Mom?"

"Asleep."

I was so tired that it felt as if my eyes weighed thousands of pounds, but I had something important that I had to say. " Daddy, please don't die. Mom and I need you. You can't leave us.''

He rubbed his rough hand over my head and smiled. "I can't promise, but I'll do my best." With that thought in my head I closed my eyes and gave myself to sleep.

The next morning was horribly hectic. Mainly because Daddy was leaving and we had a lot to do before he left. The news was last minute and had taken us all by surprise. It all started at four in the morning.

"Mint bud, wake up." My mother shook me gently and pulled back the covers. In the midst of the early morning, my room was freezing, and I wanted my blankets back. As I was getting dressed it hit me *hard* he was leaving today. At least it was only for six months, and he wasn't fighting or in a war zone. I had to stay positive.

As I got dressed in one of my usual outfits, an extra-large army t-shirt and camouflage pants, I thought of how our family would be hanging by frayed threads until he returned. He was our rock. It was summer vacation so I would be home all alone with Mom.

When I got downstairs the bright kitchen lights nearly blinded me. As my eyes adjusted, I saw my father sitting at the table eyeing the massive breakfast that my mom had prepared. Hash browns, toast, pancakes, and a fruit salad consisting of cantaloupe, honeydew, watermelon and red grapes.

My dad had a little bit of everything on his plate. He was wearing a broad smile. Two duffle bags and a suitcase with wheels were a grim reminder that he was leaving.

"Nikki, are you all right?" he asked his voice dripping with sincere concern. I nodded my head vigorously, but tears were forming in my eyes, and my throat hurt badly.

He took me into his arms, wrapped me in a strong hug, gave Mom a "hold on" signal and then took me into the living room. I was curled up beside him and crying like a fool, but it was okay; he was about to do most of the talking anyway.

"Nikki, I know you are going to miss me horribly, but I have something for you. I figured you would need this to keep you company while I was gone." He handed me a small black box that safely held a beautiful locket. Inside the locket on one side was a picture of Daddy, and on the other was a picture of he and I together. I liked it almost immediately. "Now you will have a reminder of me that can be with you at all times," he whispered so softly that I barely heard him. "I will have one as well."

He took out a small photograph; it was a recent one of me with my new haircut. "I will keep this with me, okay, and you keep the locket with you? We will never be apart."

"You have a way with words. Do you know that?" my mom asked standing in the doorway. We all laughed and headed to the kitchen to eat breakfast.

By the time breakfast was done it was time to leave. The drive to Sugartonne, the small town we lived outside, seemed to take forever. I just let my eyes glaze over and stared at the endless scenery of farm houses and lush green trees. June's series of rainfalls had been kind to the July plant life. Everything was as green as could be.

"We're here," my mom said.

I nodded and hopped down. Dad was lugging his bags toward the bus. He always had the same travel plans.

1.) Get on the Sugartonne bus
2.) Drive to Glemwood city airport
3.) Fly to destination

"Robert," my dad bellowed shaking an army man's hand.

"Long trip. Going to miss the missus?" he responded in turn.

"And Nikki."

"I'll leave you to say your goodbyes. But remember, we all have a plane to catch. The bus leaves in fifteen minutes."

"I can only do so much," Daddy said.

Mom was already crying when he came over to us, and I was doing my best not to. He looked every bit as sad as Mom and I, but his eyes held captive a glimmering shine. They only shone like that when he was really happy.

"I'm going to miss you so much," she sobbed as I stepped back to let them say goodbye.

"I'll be home before you can even miss me." He pulled her close until they were leaning against each other's foreheads. With parted lips they met in sweet seduction.

"I'll miss you, Daddy," I said.

"You too, Nikki. You be good for Mom, okay?"

"Yes, sir!"

With one final salute and a wave he boarded the bus, leaving us behind for six whole months. I tried to think positively; he looked so happy I couldn't deny him that.

"Mint bud, do you want to go home? We could pick up some ice cream. Later we could watch a movie—your pick." I nodded, and she took my hand in hers.

The drive home without him was strange but pleasant in its own way; Mom even let me sit in the front. I didn't do that very often because of the air bag. My mom made a stop at the new Sugartonne ice cream parlour. One of many parlours, bakeries, and dessert shops in Sugartonne I counted how many tiles on the roof needed to be replaced.

My mom returned just as I finished. "I got cookies 'n' cream and mint chip, homemade with extra chocolate chips. It's made with cashew milk. Do you know what movie you want to watch yet?"

"No, but fifteen shingles on that roof need to be replaced."

"You're a goof."

I didn't say much else for the rest of the way home; by the time we got there I was exhausted. My eyes were drooping, and I could feel that I was nodding off.

"You need to go back to bed, bud." My mother's voice was soothing like warm milk with the sweetness of honey. She helped me upstairs and tucked those ever so warm covers over me.

"Stay and talk with me," I begged, my voice hoarse.

She knelt down beside me and stroked my face with the arch of her fingertips. "Shhh, you need your rest."

I gave up. I couldn't protest. Darkness consumed me, and I slipped into the depths of sleep.

Two Weeks Later

Mom and I had a weekly schedule. Our schedule to communicate with Daddy.

Monday – he would phone us

Tuesday – we would email him

Wednesday – we would talk to him over webcam

Thursday – he would open our emails and email us

Friday – we would phone him

Saturday and Sunday – we would write letters

It was getting late, and I still hadn't written my letter. I had spent most of my day in the garden. We grew mostly tulips: black, red, yellow, white, all kinds. When I came in, I was covered in dirt from head to toe so Mom made me have a bath before I could do anything else. As fast as the day had begun it slipped away. So, I started my letter.

Dear Daddy,

I'm so happy every time I write to you. And I love getting your letters so much. Things are really different lately, and it feels weird with you gone. Yesterday Mom slipped and fell face first into the garden. It was funny. It would have been even funnier if you had been here to pick her up. I think it might rain. Does it rain much in Afghanistan? Have your soldiers gotten any faster with their drills? You're a good teacher. I'm sure they'll learn fast. I love you, Daddy.

Luv,

Nicole

I folded up the paper and slipped it safely into the envelope. The mini clock on the table read 9:03 p.m. Mom was shuffling around in the living room probably getting ready for our Saturday movie. We were watching a nature documentary about the cats in Africa.

I gasped in astonishment when I saw what my mom had set up. The couch was extra cushiony with a black velvet comforter and a silky blue quilt with patches of blue covering both sides. As if that wasn't good enough she had lined the glossy glass table with bowls of popcorn, ice cream, Coke floats, and black forest cake.

"Movie's going to start soon, bud. Do you like everything?"

"I love it."

We curled up under the soft blankets and let our eyes relax while we gazed at the magnificent African scenery and regal animals. Our movie was soon interrupted by a ring at the door.

"Excuse me, my wife and baby are injured. May we please use your phone?"

My mom's face went pale, and her eyes clouded she recognized the man through the window glass, and whoever he was, he was obviously frightening her. "Honey, go upstairs and phone 911."

"Why?"

"Just do it," she hissed.

I was halfway up the stairs when a loud crack froze me dead in my tracks. The glass window on the door had been shattered, and two men forced their way inside. I managed to scramble up the rest of the stairs and hide behind the thick railing. The two men walked tauntingly around Mother. "Do you remember us? Why don't we introduce ourselves to jog your memory?"

The first man wore his thick blonde hair slicked back with some sort of gel. He was of average height and probably in his early twenties. His other features appeared to be perfect, brilliantly white teeth and rich blue eyes.

The other one looked like he could be his brother. He seemed to be a few years younger and looked completely different. His scraggly dirty brown hair the colour of milk chocolate was tied back in a greasy ponytail. He looked frightening; his eyes were dark and clouded, and on his bottom tooth was a golden cap that glinted when he talked.

Mom was obviously in severe distress. I needed to do everything in my power to help her and I needed to get to the only phone in the house, which was upstairs. But the men could easily see me if I ran to the other side of the staircase.

I tried so hard to move quickly, but I stumbled. Before I knew what was happening I rolled down the top three stairs. My sweaty fingers barely grasped the smooth white stair railing.

"Nicole, run," my mother screamed frantically. "Get away from them. Run." The younger one grabbed her arms and pulled her away from me. She kicked and screamed but couldn't break free.

The older one slowly walked toward me. "What's your name, little girl?"

"Nicole," I said hesitantly. I wasn't sure what he would do if I didn't answer.

He took my hands and offered a tender smile. "Your hands are so small and delicate."

"Let me go." I tried to pull away, but his grip tightened, and in a flash of silver he pulled out a surprisingly small pair of glistening silvery handcuffs, and I was cuffed securely to the railing. "No," I yelled.

"Get ready," he said gesturing to his brother.

"To do what, Nicholas?"

"Just do what I say, Kevin," the older one replied.

Nicholas wouldn't answer me, but he did un-cuff me. I pulled as hard as I possibly could to get away or break free, but it only resulted in me getting re-cuffed to the bottom step.

"Mommy," I cried in horror. Kevin was holding a sharp long triangular pointed knife to her throat. The two men stood over her. They started at her feet binding them with thick white ropes to our solid antique table. There was no way she could pull away; it was too heavy.

Then they moved up to her arms. Kevin smiled. "I'll take the left. You do the right, Nicholas." Nick nodded. He took her wrist and in a slow motion twisted it backward until a sickening crack echoed through the air breaking the haunting silence, followed by my mother's moans of pain. She was gagged so she couldn't scream. Her arm hung at an awkward angle. It was badly broken.

"Leave her alone," I screamed helplessly. My fear worsened as the man named Nicholas squatted down beside her taking the knife from his brother. I was even more helpless as he sunk the blade deep into my mother's skin. An amazingly bright stream of blood broke out soaking her skin and running down her arm and torso. Tears of fear and pain shed down her face. The more I tried to pull away the more the handcuffs dug into my skin and cut me.

"Nicole, stop struggling. It's useless." Nicholas spoke softly and gently. "I'm going to tell you a little rhyme, and you are going to keep your eyes on me."

"Let my mom go."

"That's not possible now."

I managed to peer over his shoulder and see her poor condition. Her eyes were dark, and she had laboured breathing. Each breath that she took seemed to be a whole new struggle. Half of her body was completely red with blood.

Nicholas moved closer to me, and I could no longer see her. "I'm going to tell you the rhyme, and you are going to keep your eyes on me.

A-B-C, one two three

She has to die, don't you cry

Slit her throat on this note

Blood comes out, out about

She is dead all nice and red."

"It's done," Kevin said wiping his hands on his jeans, which were soaked. As both men moved away my eyes bulged in horror; she was dead.

Nicholas released me from the awful handcuffs, and I ran to her body.

"Mom," I sobbed. "Mommy, wake up." I tugged on her fingers. They lifted up, then down. She was alive! With a much-laboured movement she took my hand and squeezed. I could tell she was trying to talk to me, but only a low moan escaped her torn open throat.

"Uh, Nick, she's still alive."

My brain went into self-defence mode. I needed to get upstairs and phone 911. Two problems stood in my path—Mom's almost murderers, Nicholas and Kevin.

Kevin started toward me holding a simple Exacto knife in his trembling hand. Before he could react I kicked him in his shins and snatched the knife as he dropped it. Neither of them could grab me as I bolted up the stairs. I almost made it, but Kevin caught up to me, grabbed my ankle and dragged me down.

I rolled over on my stomach shielding the knife. "Give it to me, bitch." He kicked my ribs as hard as he could, and my whole body shook. Pain shot from my head to feet.

"Kevin, get the knife."

"I'm trying, idiot."

Nicholas laughed. "Roll her over."

He tried to flip me, but I shoved the knife deep into his arm. He screeched in pain. "She just stabbed me."

"Calm down, Kevin. You know you are stupid as shit." He knelt down beside me. "Are you going to give me the knife?"

I attempted stabbing him, but I missed and felt a sharp prick as a needle jutted out of my wrist. Their faces slowly blurred into a collection of pixels and then faded into shadows until I saw nothing, nothing but unsettling darkness.

It felt as if a couple of seconds later I was up and awake. Everything on my body hurt especially my ribs. I struggled to stand up, but my feet were bound, and I was cuffed again this time to a metal pole. It hurt to breathe. Each breath I took smelled like dirt. I was in some underground cellar where the walls were crumbly brown with a dirt like substance, and there were sets of twinkly lights on them. Some bulbs were chipped and cracked while others shone brightly.

"You're awake," Nicholas said softly.

My eyes watered, and I couldn't see him clearly. I couldn't even think of what he looked like. "What's wrong with me?"

"You're drugged."

"Why did you kill my mother?"

"You don't want to know."

"Yes, I do," I demanded trying to sound fierce, but to him I was about as scary as a pussy cat.

"Well, a couple of years ago when your father was in Afghanistan he killed our youngest brother, Luke."

"My mother shouldn't have had to pay the price."

"Your father shouldn't have killed Luke."

"He probably deserved to die. Daddy doesn't randomly kill people—you do. My dad killed terrorists. I bet that's what Luke was—a black-hearted terrorist that murdered innocent people."

His eyes clouded, and his jaw had tightened. Before I knew what was happening he punched me in the eye with such force I banged my head on the wall and dirt crumbled loose into my hair.

With my free hand I wiped away a mixture of blood and tears. The hit was so powerful even my nose dripped with blood, and even though I was in a lot of pain I managed to force the words out. "Are you going to kill me too?"

I didn't get my answer, just another needle. This time though when I woke up they were gone. I looked down. I was wearing white, and everything around me looked white also. Walls, lights, even the people were clothed in white uniforms. Was I in heaven?

"Where am I?" I manage to croak. My voice was hoarse.

"Honey, you're in the hospital," answered an unfamiliar doctor. I was surprised Nicholas and Kevin had let me go; I had witnessed their crime.

A police officer with long straight black hair and slanted eyes approached me. "Nicole, your mother is dead."

"I know," I replied sounding more than ever like a robot. I must have been in shock. I couldn't feel anything.

"Do you think you could come with me to answer some questions? Do you feel up to it?"

It felt like she was already asking me enough questions, and answers were not coming easily. "I'm sore," I said feeling exhausted, but I still got down from the bed.

The young doctor smiled down at me. "You're one tough girl."

The officer took my hand, and we walked slowly and carefully to her special police car. When she leaned over to buckle me in, I could see that she smelled like flowers like our garden. The drive was short, and in no time, I was sitting in a cushiony chair being gawked at by strangers. I wanted Daddy. At this moment, I needed a hug.

Slanted eyes lady soon came back with her partner. He had slicked down carrot red hair. For the first time since the hospital, she introduced herself. "Well, Nicole, my name is Agent. Sen, and this is my partner Agent Bell. We're going to ask you a couple of questions."

They sat me down in a room that had a very soft comfy chair but too bright of a light, which hurt my eyes.

That's when the questions started.

Who took you?

What did they look like?

Where is your father?

What does your father do for a living?

Do you know the men that took you?

Did they mention a last name?

How did they kill your mother?

They went on and on. I almost started crying from all of the pressure. I couldn't remember who took me or picture their faces. I could still hear their voices in my mind and feel them beating me. I knew that there was one way that I could remember: I had to recite the rhyme.

"Wait, don't go," I cried as they stood at the door fiddling with their keys to let themselves out. "I know something that might help. I may even be able to give you a description."

They returned to their seats quick as lightning. "What do you remember?" Agent Bell urged.

"It's a rhyme," I answered so softly that my voice was barely audible.

"Tell us," they said in unison.

"A-B-C, one two three

She has to die, don't you cry

Slit her throat on this note

Blood comes out, out about

She is dead all nice and red."

Then I remembered every sick twisted thing they did to her and to me. Words spilled out of my mouth until I had told my whole story, and I was left with just one question: "Where am I going to spend the night?"

"We're still trying to find you a place. We have a nice worker who is going to keep you company while we find you a place," Agent Sen explained soothingly.

And speak of the devil, there she was. She looked official wearing a tanned suit, matching skirt, and neat sandy brown hair pinned neatly up in a bun.

"Hello, Nicole. My name is Christine. I am sorry for your loss."

I stared at her, puzzled. "It wasn't your fault."

She uttered an awkwardly forced laugh, and her face turned beet red. "Well, no, I suppose not; do you mind coming with me?"

"No, I don't mind."

She took my hand and led me to another room with two long black couches that looked as if they belonged in a psychiatrist's office.

Christine faked a far too phony smile. "We're going to find you a good place."

"I'm not an orphan, and I'm not stupid. So, can you stop? I just want my dad."

She just sat there for several moments as if I had stopped her. Then ignoring everything I had just said the voice returned: "Would you like something to eat?"

"No."

"Nicole, I have to go. Serena will pick you up shortly."

"Where are you going?"

"I have a meeting to attend to." Her voice wasn't as nice now.

The door clicked shut behind her, and the room darkened. I don't think I had ever felt so alone. Mom was dead. Daddy was probably on a plane coming home, but he wouldn't be here until tomorrow. For now, I was the child no one wanted.

"Nicole."

At first I thought it was Christine, but a younger woman with long white-blonde hair and a gentle voice stood over me. It must have been Serena.

"Oh, sweetheart." She climbed down beside me and rubbed my back. "There, there, let it out." Her light blue eyes watered sympathetically; she cared about me. She would help me.

"Do you know where I am going to stay?" I asked choking on sobs.

"We found a nice couple, country folk Mr. and Mrs. Trent."

"Are they here?"

"They're waiting right outside."

Two strangers awaited my arrival. Mrs. Trent had a tired face, but her soft brown eyes were warm and comforting. She was dressed simply wearing a faded blue dress, with her hair pinned up. Her husband, on the other hand, looked strong. His dark eyes were large and seemed to go with the rest of his stern chiselled features. His dark brown beard was thick and round.

"You look mighty tired, dear," he said in a deep voice.

Mrs. Trent stroked my face. "You need some rest, and we should put some food in that empty belly."

The couple nodded at me. She took my hand, and they led me to a rusted brown pick-up truck. As I peered into the back seat, I noticed there was no seatbelt. Instead there were a worn blue quilt and a white pillow.

"Just lay down, sweetie. The drive isn't that long," Mrs. Trent said. I was too tired to protest.

I guess I had dozed off because the next thing I knew, we were stopped at an all wooded house. "Nicole, we're here." Mrs. Trent stood over me: "I had my husband get your room and snack ready."

"Okay." I sighed. With a bit of effort I managed to make my way inside the house. "What time is it?"

"I don't think I've ever been this tired."

She chuckled softly. "Well, you don't have to go any farther. Here is the room you'll be staying in." The room was a cozy kind of perfect. A bed made with nice blue blankets and a large extravagant wooden table with elaborate details. And to the right was a large stained glass window.

On the table rested my snack: a slice of buttered bread that appeared to be homemade and a tall glass of milk.

Soon Mrs. Trent had me snuggled into bed as good as my own mother could. The bread was delicious—light and fluffy with the salty taste of butter. To wash it down I let the warm milk flow like a river down my throat.

"You've been through so much in one night. You know, I lost my mother when I was about your age."

"How?"

"The doctors couldn't figure out what was wrong with her, and one day she just died."

"Oh."

"But my father made everything really easy for me, and I'm sure your dad will too." She added with a thoughtful glance, "Good night, Nicole."

When I woke up, early morning sun streaked into the room. The whole area around the bed was lit with light. Once again, I was hungry. I hoped Mrs. Trent could make me something to eat before we went to the airport.

The kitchen smelled pleasantly of porridge "I made you breakfast." She scooped a heaping pile of brown sugar on the mound. I smiled to myself. This was just what I wished for.

"Where's your husband?"

"At work," she replied.

I grinned at the sugary taste of my sweetened meal. I ate quickly and finished as fast as I could.

"You all ready to go?"

I nodded rapidly. The sooner we left, the sooner I could be back with Daddy. The phone rang suddenly breaking the moment of silence.

"Just a minute, dear," Mrs. Trent said as she picked up the phone.

"Who was that?" I asked when she hung up.

"That was Agent Sen. Your father absolutely insists that he will pick you up here."

Worried thoughts race through my mind. "How will he find me?"

"He has the directions."

"Oh, okay."

She smiled pleasantly and took a seat beside me "You are one brave girl."

"I'm not that brave."

"You've been through so much, and I haven't even seen one little tear in those beautiful eyes."

"I cried when he hit me."

"Well, that beast did a number on your eye."

My hand shot to my face. I could feel the actual swelling around it. "What exactly does it look like?"

"You haven't seen it? Well, I guess I'll just have to show you."

She handed me a small mirror. I gasped in shock. My whole eye was black and swollen. Broken blood vessels made the narrow visible strip of it look blood red. I was a mess. Then there was a completely awful silence that was broken by the sudden rumble of a truck's engine. Daddy!!!

I bolted out the door and fell scraping my face on the gravel.

"Nikki!"

I wiped a bleeding cut on my jeans and climbed to my feet. "You're back."

"What happened to your eye?"

"The man hit it."

He scooped me up into his arms and held me tight "We're going to be all right."

I climbed down and stepped back as Mrs. Trent came out. "I am so sorry for your loss. May our lord God be with you."

"Thank you."

"Are we going home?" I asked anxiously.

"No, Nikki, we have a new place to live."

Chapter Two

Ten Years Later

My large mirror offered a blurred image of my early morning reflection. I suppose it was vain, but over the years I had blossomed into an exquisite creature as my father called me. Crewcut blonde hair, lightly tanned skin, large deep hazel eyes and an average built body.

Since my mother died, or as I should say was murdered, life was very different. First we moved to the mountains a couple hours north of Sugartonne. That was mainly because of Dad's new job. Well, it wasn't really new. He still trained soldiers, but it was here in rocky isolation.

There was hardly anyone who lived here. Maybe fewer than twenty people made homes here in cottages similar to our own. Miss Parker, my private teacher, was one of them. I was one of the only residents that still required schooling, and she was the only teacher.

We tended to be the only people that occupied the red-brick school house.

"God, I'm late," I cried with a sudden shriek. My digital wrist watch read 7:58. I was supposed to be at school already or at least walking there.

As I jumped down from my bed, which was slightly raised, my ankle still tender throbbed with excruciating pain. Due to an annoyingly deep pot hole, in my dad's words, I had a nasty sprain.

I threw on one of my usual outfit's—tee-shirt and camouflage pants all while fumbling aimlessly for my crutches.

I slipped an apple and a bottle of water into my bag along with a sandwich I made last night, making my best attempt to get out the door past the watchful eyes of Dad. Failure.

"You know you're late," he said without looking up from his computer screen.

"You could have woken me up."

"I won't be here forever. Didn't you set your alarm?"

"Maybe."

"Hey, don't leave yet. Take a jacket."

"Yes sir," I replied sarcastically.

"I do not enjoy sarcasm."

I giggled and slipped on my forest green silk jacket.

"Bye."

"Have a good day, Nikki."

I hobbled along the upwards sloping trail. It was at least a twenty minute walk. The October air was brisk and cool. We didn't really get much snow here; it hardly ever got cold enough to snow. Trees dense with the colours of red orange and yellow were scattered everywhere reminding me of that.

Eventually, the large school house with its faded red bricks and old fashioned appearance came into view.

The door squealed loudly as usual. Just like my dad, Miss Parker said the same thing. "You're late." Her voice was stern, and even though she wasn't looking at me, I could feel the sting of her blue eyes, which were cold as ice. When she was joyous they were sparkly. But if you made her cross they seemed to burn your flesh.

"Please accept my apology, ma'am. I slept late, and on this ankle, it's hard to get around." I let my voice trail off.

"I'll accept that reason this time, but any more tardiness and I'll have to have a meeting with your father."

"Yes, ma'am."

"Nicole, you may lose the formality. I'm not going to eat you." Her voice lightened, and she smiled. She had a beautiful smile.

I laughed lightly. Miss Parker was a great teacher. She was smart, funny, kind, and attractive. Her peachy blonde hair was seldom down, but I knew it was almost past her waistline. Her blue eyes were framed with thick lashes, and she had the clearest skin I had ever seen.

"So what are we doing today?"

"Well, we're going to do something a little different. I want you to do a writing assignment.

Write anything you like, but you have to get your idea from one word."

"Which word?"

"Winter."

I smiled. This day was going to go by very fast. A story was already writing itself in my mind.

The Tale of a Girl Named Winter
Written by Nicole

I am human. My name is Winter, or at least I think it is. For many months my parents have been gone, and since then two things have happened: it hasn't stopped snowing, and I haven't eaten. These are two things that have to be explained and can't just be said.

The first January out of nowhere it started to snow. White, white, and more white. The ground lost its green; trees became gnarled and bare from the cold. It used to be warm with lots of heat from the sun, but when the clouds came, they covered it almost every hour of every day. Even if they were blown away by the harsh winds, the sun shone grey. Its light was too bleak and full of despair to lay eyes upon.

Over time my parents started to neglect me; their obsession with trying to bring colour to the fading place grew. Each day they planted flowers only for the full grown ones to die or seeds to never sprout. They tried everything they could to bring colour back or stop the snow.

When they couldn't fix their home, they turned their anger on me. "You're the winter's source. You bring the ice," my mother would scream over and over again.

As for my father he didn't yell, but his love for me vanished. I was no longer a flesh and blood seventeen-year-old girl—now I was the winter.

I stared out my windows into the endless blur of white and begged silently for the light to return. But one day when I woke up, and it was snowing harder than ever, my parents were gone without a trace.

At that point, the most solemn moment in my life I realized that I was no longer a loved happy child. I was the cursed winter whom my parents thought would die in this house. But as the food ran out and the water containers were bone dry, I drank from the small drips of icicles that replenished my thick tongue thirst. For months that was all I required. It did not give me the nutrients that food would have, though.

My ribs jutted out sharply. My arms and legs took the same appearance as thin, brittle twigs. The lengthy weeks without attention took their toll, and my already long white-blonde hair grew until I could wrap it around my ankles.

And then everything changed. Until you came, I was alone. You showed up suddenly like the snow itself. I thought you were my angel, the guardian who would save me from this frozen hell.

You were very attractive. Blonde hair, thick and wavy, fell into your face concealing much of your pale skin and heartless blue eyes.

"Help me," I said over and over.

You would not answer my desperate pleas but continued to pace still wearing a sadistic smile. "Come with me," you said.

"Will you help me?"

"Help you? I'm going to kill you."

My rush of relief turned to fear. I couldn't react before the white faded and the room turned to black; shadows loomed menacingly in every corner.

"Let me go," I screamed desperately, my voice echoing continually off the stone walls until my throat burned with pain.

You continued to look at me intently narrowing your eyes with every step I took. You placed a tray of buttered bread and milky tea at my feet, watching me eat with a sick smile on your face. I ate so fast the bread stuck in my throat.

A flash of silver whizzed through the air, and blood poured from my throat. I lay on the floor helpless taking my final breaths as the light consumed me.
The end

"Miss Parker," I said laying my pencil to rest. "I've finished."

"Very good, Nicole. I say that you've fulfilled your goal and created a well-lengthened story, but of course the real treat will be reading your work."

A hollow pain filled me as she took the papers, and my eyes stole a second glance at the inky dreary words, words that did not fit in my mouth.

"Is something wrong, dear?"

"Oh, nothing, ma'am."

"Nicole," she snapped. "Do not lie to me." Her face then softened. "I know when something is troubling you."

"Well, I know this is going to sound strange, but my story, the one that I just wrote, the words just don't fit in my mouth. It sounds like someone gave me the idea."

"Meaning you plagiarized it."

"No." I searched my mind for the right words. "Um, it was like the words just came."

"I'm sure you just had an inspiration. Perhaps you are destined to write."

"What time is it?"

"It's almost two. I suppose you can head home."

I nodded silently as I collected my books. It was as if the entire time I was writing, I was forced into a trance. The ideas in my mind turning to words; none of it belonged to me. The strangest thing was that it all seemed to be true, but it was also all logically impossible.

How had time slipped away so fast? The story wasn't that long. It was a mere few pages. I could feel Miss Parker's eyes on me, hard, like burning coals, so I forced a smile and fumbled aimlessly for my crutches. My heavy wooden chair tipped slowly with a rickety creak, and as I tried to regain my balance—SPLAT. I was on the floor tasting dust and splinters.

"Nicole?" Miss Parker said.

"Whoops, I'm okay." I turned my back quickly and limped out of the room the best I could. Even as the autumn wind whipped my face offering cool relaxation, I was still tense with questions.

How did I take so long to write the story?
Why did I feel pain?
How did I write it?
If the words aren't mine whose are they?

A male voice broke my thoughts. "I know you, Nicole."

"Who are you?"

"Why should I tell you?" he replied.

"Who the hell is this?"

"Don't worry. After I kill you I'll meet you in *hell.*"

My whole body shook, and my hands trembled so badly that my crutches nearly slipped. My eyes darted back and forth looking for the person who had spoken to me but to no avail. I was almost halfway home. Was it too risky? Should I go back to Miss Parker? But would she even believe me, for I had not seen a person? Not many people lived here. I knew almost everyone, and I was positive no one new had come. I shook my head and continued down. Perhaps I was imagining things, yet it seemed so real and frightening, vivid and shocking. During the rest of the way home, I heard no more voices.

"Did you have a nice day?" My dad greeted me as the door opened. Despite the disturbing walk home his deep voice and friendly smile easily comforted me

"Yes, it was all right." I was not going to tell him. I didn't see anyone. Maybe I had imagined the voice.

"Well, I hope you're hungry. Because I brought home a bucket load of groceries."

I had had a brief lunch at school: a plain peanut butter sandwich with no jam. It was a boring sandwich that I prepared myself; I did not have the gift to prepare fine cuisine or even simple meals. Now I felt famished. "I'm ravenous."

He placed a tray of warm, extra gooey brownies, in front of me. Chocolate chips bulged out the sides, and a thick drizzle of icing covered the whole top. They tasted even better than they looked. Warm and creamy with a sweet aftertaste as they slid down my throat. They disappeared awfully quickly, too quickly.

Later that evening we sat in our living room eating portabella mushrooms. My dad had discovered a new thing. These weird giant mushrooms tasted just like steaks when seasoned right. I felt scared as if something horrible was about to happen. Even my delicious well-done mushroom steak and flashing television couldn't distract me, so I called it a night and went to bed early.

"Nicole, I'm worried about you. You've been acting strange since you got home. Did the baker drug those brownies? Have I given my daughter fruit of the poison tree?"

I laughed bitterly. "No, I think I'm just a little down."

"Well, maybe I'll talk Miss Parker into letting you stay home."

"No," I cried anxiously. The last thing I needed was to be stuck at home. "I'll be fine."

"You sure?" he asked.

"Absolutely."

"Okay, then. Good night, Nikki."

"Night, Dad."

He flicked the hallway light off, and as I went into my room I closed my eyes trying to relax. I felt bone dead tired, but I was not at all sleepy, so I grabbed my reading light and reached for a cheesy romance novel I had been reading. It had a lot of clichés, but the plot was nice, and the characters had their strengths. But instead of feeling my book I felt a piece of loose-leaf paper. A letter. Curious to see what it was I turned my reading light to its highest setting and let my eyes skim.

Dear anyone,

Once when I picked up a pen, it did not feel like it weighed a thousand pounds. Once I was as normal as normal could be. Once I was happy. Once I was a normal sixteen-year-old girl.

But as time wore on and I turned seventeen, then the snow came on a random January. My parents left, and the man I thought was my angel took both me and then my life.

- but Nicole, you know the rest
- you're going to meet me
- winter in
- hell. Enjoy your life in the meantime.

My story had a girl named Winter and the man who had killed her. I was now positive the voice that I had heard, the man that I had spoken to, was the man in the story. He couldn't be a man though because he wasn't mortal.

Chapter Three

My eyes refused to stay open, and I fell into a stomach-churning nightmare.

"It's so nice to see you again, Nicole," said the man who had spoken to me earlier, the one I had not seen.

When I tried to stand up, leather restraints dug into my wrists and ankles. A hard cold slab of a metal table pressed itself against my back. I was clothed in a black bikini that barely covered my breasts.

"Let me go."

"I'm not physically holding you captive. You're locked in the realm of your own mind. This is your nightmare."

"What kind of sick bastard are you?"

"Nicole doesn't speak to me that way. You're breaking my heart. I want you."

I pulled harder on the straps, but they cut my wrists. Sharp glistening silver blades stuck into my skin and pierced the flesh sending a stream of blood down to my feet.

He continued to speak to me, his voice a false soothing tone. His steel blue eyes were all I could see of him. "Nikki, relax baby. Such a beautiful creature should not be so afraid."

I could feel a light hand on my shoulder, but the touch was far from gentle. Once I was stung by a wasp. The pain I had felt then was horrific; him touching me was like a thousand wasps stinging me. Tears of pain shed rapidly down my face; I could feel his presence still hovering over me.

"Awake now."

The next thing I knew I was sitting upright in bed, my tearstained face dripping with sweat. Blankets were thrown everywhere and even wrapped around my neck. It made no sense. How had I felt pain? It was a nightmare: one that felt very real, though. Droplets of blood clung to my arm unwilling to move. As my eyes travelled downwards, they revealed a black rose entwined through my fingers. Perhaps I should have gotten my dad, but he wouldn't have believed me.

What was I supposed to do? Tell him that an immortal creature, maybe a vampire, attacked me while I was locked in a realm of my own nightmare? And he also spoke to me on the way home. All the while I received a letter from the dead girl, Winter, whom I had written a disturbing story about. Maybe I should even mention that we should meet in hell. Oh no, that doesn't sound crazy at all. I spent hours awake before I drifted into another sleep full of empty darkness.

When I woke up this time earlier and ready to go to school without rushing I found a letter sitting on my dresser.

Dear family and friends,

I know ever so well that you will be devastated when you find my body hanging from this noose, a noose made of fraying white rope that has seen better days. I cannot continue on with my life that is so dreary and full of darkness. Each time I close my eyes I envision dogs with slit throats and cats torn to shreds, their heads in once piece, their bloodshot eyes bulging outwards. I can't sleep due to nightmares and stress that tears at my stomach. Mother, I know you will miss me, but you still have John, Emily, and Dad. They can still give you all the happiness you need. For my two friends, Lexie and Samantha, be strong. I would have only dragged you farther down the social ladder. The two of you have the energy to live. I do not.

If you do not understand why I would do this, I have other reasons. For a long time now, at least over a year, something has hovered over me. I could not tell anyone, though or the results would have been terrible. You all would have locked me up in a mental hospital or made me see a therapist who would talk about all the junk my mind does, and you would not have believed my story one little bit. The pain nags at you a little each day until one day you just snap. Or the pain returns. Time heals no wounds because eventually, every haunting memory comes back worse than before. Again over and over and over and over and over and over.

This is why I cannot move forward with my past and also the present, which is also hurting me.

Signed, your once moonlit daughter

"Dad," I screamed as loud as I could. My hands shook so badly I couldn't even hold the letter. "Dad."

No answer. Great, he must have gone to work early as I ventured downstairs where I found a note on the kitchen table.

Nikki, had to go to work early. It's going to be a busy day. I'll probably be home late so don't wait up. Love you.

And so there I was left at home all alone staring at two pieces of paper, their cruel words and individual letters taunting me. All I had left was school.

School was no better. I heard the man mock me all day long.

Me: "Leave me alone."
Him: "Why should I?"
Me: "What do you want?"
Him: "I want you."
Me: "Why me?"
Him: "You're special. Do you doubt yourself? I know I don't doubt you."
Me: "LEAVE."

But the battle raged on in my head, and it went on for two weeks from home to school and back again with this strange voice stalking me until I had one week off while Miss Parker attended meetings in Glemwood. When I was off my father was the exact opposite. He worked almost all day, and some nights he didn't even get home at night. For six whole days of my extended weekend, I heard nothing of the strange man and only found one note.

Dear Nicole,

I live in a horrible hell like place constantly being watched by the keepers that have chosen to guard me. Of course, you do not understand this, but one day you will. Let me say actually, someday you will, and that day will come soon. This letter is a hard one to write but, oh, I don't know. Just know this. I know your fate will be one that is strange.
Signed by a female who prefers to be left anonymous

Instead of spending the rest of my last day off moping around, all alone, worrying about the immortal force haunting me I decided to spend my day outside.

A worn-out path that was mainly used to get up to the top of the mountain led to small clearings that were particularly pleasant and warm even in later fall. I probably shouldn't have been doing so much walking since my ankle was still very sore, but I needed to get away. At least I wasn't on crutches anymore, which made it easier to walk. I went higher and higher until my ankle hurt so badly that I stopped by a large oak tree to rest. The forest floor surrounding it was scattered with large ripe acorns and pleasant smelling serrated edged leaves. A nice spot to stop and rest.

A warm breeze touched my skin and blew the earthy dirt concoction of leaves and browning crisp grass into my face. I sneezed loudly and slightly startled myself. As minutes turned to hours, I just sat there breathing in the fresh mountain air. All my stresses and worries vanished. But the daylight faded eventually, and darkness overwhelmed me. I limped down the trail to a dark house. Dad wasn't home yet. Letting myself in I slipped through the dark and up to my room.

Desperate to escape the gloomy blackness I flipped on every light that my room had. Eight o'clock and I had nothing to do. I could phone Dad, but he'd be too busy. I could read, but I had already read all the good books. There was TV, but nothing but junk was on.

Then out of the yellow mist a luminous light my lamp created floated a dark blue envelope sealed with a wax seal. All of the letters I had found were written on the loose-leaf paper. This letter was completely different in absolutely every detail. Besides the envelope the paper was different too. It was beige and had a slightly bumpy texture to it. The sharp edges cut my hands when I removed it from the envelope. Even the words were different. They were inky neat and spiralled as if written by that of a calligraphy pen.

It read: Addressed to Nicole Aloevere—I have watched you all of your life, and I know every detail about you. My cousin has sent you many letters, but I have not. I must inform you that many people want to kill you. I have no interest in that matter, and when I claim you as my eternal fair maiden your blood will stain my hands, and you will be my slave from now and forever more.

A lack of energy and sleepiness overwhelmed me from out of nowhere. I lay on my bed breathing heavily but barely conscious. Something ran across my neck, and I saw a hint of blue eyes, but they faded to a vivid green. Lighter than emeralds but just as powerful and majestic. My fingers tingled, but I could not move my hand. All the strength I previously had was drained from my body. As my eyes closed and I saw the eyes still green watching me. I could hear voices, murmuring whispers, helpless pleas.

The lights went out, and hair brushed against my face. How was that even possible? I hadn't had long hair since I was six.

As I opened my eyes very slowly and cautiously, I looked at the bright light surrounding me. The sun that held a firm position in the high sky was the brightest I had ever seen, its light so warm and radiant it made my skin tingle. My hand brushed my silky fabric as I stretched out. What I felt was a dress. As I stood up the blackness of its fabric fell past my ankles. It was unlike anything I had ever worn. A tight corset pushed my sides inward, but it did not feel awkward nor uncomfortable overall. It was rather light and soft.

My feet hurt terribly as I stood up. They were covered in open bleeding blisters that were quite red and swollen. Blood stained the lush grass as I walked. The land was so green it stretched for miles in all directions with seemingly no end.

A chocolaty light brown rabbit scampered out from a cluster of flowers nearby. It startled me as if I were an illegal alien, but as it hopped by me and its fur soft as dandelions brushed against my feet the blisters vanished. I reached down to stroke it, but before my fingers had even reached near it, it ran back into the safety of the flowers.

"Well, that's odd," I said aloud, but my voice seemed so small in this vast empty place. Just then it occurred to me I may have been dreaming.

"Nicole, someone is trying to kill you," someone said without emotion.

And then there I was sitting upright in bed sweating like a pig slaughtered. "It was just a dream," I said trying to reassure myself and calm my rapidly beating heart. The sound of my voice was already putting me back to sleep, and just as I realized this, I knew I was falling into another nightmare.

There was straw on the ground, and the four walls that surrounded me were made of rotting damp wood that smelled like mould.

My shoulder was twisted at an awkward angle and ached horribly. It throbbed and was soaked with sticky clumps of drying blood. A long hooked blade was embedded in my skin. Several grunts and loud snorts forced me to come to my senses. I saw pigs. Three of them were walking around the room.

The first one was a very light whitish colour and had a creamy face; the poor sow had swollen nipples, and her ribs were so pointy. They looked as if they could cut you, even if you barely touched them.

The second sow was not any better. Her pretty pink colour was not nearly as eerie as the first one, but still, she looked worse. Her mouth dripped with a thick mixture of foamy blood and saliva, and her hooves were chipped and cracked. Every step she took, she groaned wincing in pain.

Finally, there was a creamy white one with a black patch over her eye. At first, I thought she was healthy until she turned to me, and I saw that her eyes were bleak, hopeless, and dreary. They were also much clouded; I assumed she was blind. But that was not what was disturbing me. Below her left eye, the flesh torn in a jagged patch hung down; the open wound was crawling with thick fat maggots that sucked on the blood. She lifted her head with a cry of pain, and several maggots fell down from the pig's face.

I mentally named them all:

Piggy one – Missy
Piggy two-– Blossom
Piggy three – Patch

I reached out and gently rubbed Missy's face. Her eyes relaxed, and she sighed happily. It must've been a very long time since these poor three animals had ever been loved or shown attention. Rain bounced off the makeshift metal roof and leaked through the boards. Ping, ping, ping. Over and over it sounded as if we were being attacked.

A door at the far side of the room that I hadn't noticed opened slowly with the loud creak.

An African American man with dreads and very dark narrow eyes entered like a spirit slave to the dead. "Pigs and an ugly wretch pinned to the wall. How the world makes such ugly creatures I do not know."

Missy, Blossom, and Patch made a semi-circle around me. They were trying to protect me. The man snorted in disgust. "Stupid animals. No point on this earth but to make meat. Exactly what you'll be doing, little girl."

Out of the shadows curled in his fingers rested a rusty axe tipped with blood. With Missy in front of me, Patch on my right and Blossom on my left I was well surrounded but not for long. He raised the axe and sent it flying down breaking Missy's face in half. A strange noise escaped her mouth, and as the blood poured her head fell in half. She had had been struck dead. The large pool of blood crept up to my ankles staining my warm flesh; a cold sweat broke out on my face.

High squeals of pain and desperation broke the awful silence. Both pigs stared mournfully at their dead companion. Still, they refused to leave my side.

He would not stop. The axe held a rare shine and came down to my throat. "No," I screamed helplessly as a slicing pain seared through my throat. Instead of meeting endless darkness or a golden gate I was staring straight at a desk scattered with loose-leaf papers. A desk, a bookshelf, my old stuffed bunny Choco. My room. I was home. I was safe.

"You're not safe, Nicole," a man said sadistically as a dagger made of gold slipped through the darkness.

Chapter Four

No, no, this could not be happening. I could hear the sound of his voice clearly and feel the dagger as it trailed down my arm.

"Nikki, what's wrong?"

"Get the hell away from me." I jerked my legs back and kicked as hard as I could, but I missed and felt only air as two strong hands pinned me down. "No, let me go."

"Shhh, Nikki. It's me."

"Dad."

"What's wrong? You were screaming."

"I had a really bad nightmare," I said.

"Okay, I'll go downstairs and fix you the usual remedy."

"All right." The usual remedy was warm milk, my mom's favourite old blanket, and a piece of chocolate. I grabbed my gold house coat and left to my relaxation. When I got downstairs, everything was set up just as it always was.

"What's happening?" he asked gently. "Why are you having nightmares?" I sipped the milk anxiously. It burned my tongue. Everything I had kept secret for the past week came tumbling out. The letters, the voices, the story, all the details, everything.

I searched my father's face for any signs of emotional distress, fear, anxiety, disbelief, anything, but he looked the same as always.

"Do you have any of these letters?" he asked calmly.

"Yes, yes, they're on my dresser." I ran as fast as I could stumbling up the stairs, but my excitement turned to horror when I saw that the letters were ………… Gone!!

Blood was pooling around my chair. "I'm going to lock you away. You'll never see your father ever again. I hoped you liked that short little letter. This is me now." I saw a cold hint of green eyes.

"Nikki, calm down," my father yelled.

"They're not here. The letters are gone."

In an act of rage I grabbed the desk and landed so hard on it the leg snapped, and the details of a spiralled supporter cut me.

"Take a deep breath." He grabbed me and pulled me upwards. His grip was so strong I had never felt it like that because not once in my life had he ever been so forceful with me. Then he stuck a needle in my arm. It was a sedative that he had used at work in training exercises.

Yellow flashing circles danced around me. Then green, then blue, then black, all dark.

Two women hovered around me. They appeared to be made of nothing more than misty wispy shadows that wavered and drifted. Their faces looked gothic with a dark angelic glow. Hair that touched the floor was soft and silky brushing against my face.

"Come with us, Nicole," they hissed in unison. I attempted to grab something as one of the women scraped her piercing nails against my skin.

"We'll drag you to hell slowly!" one sneered with a sadistic smile on her face.

"No, Dad. Help me!" I tried and tried to reach out to him. But he wasn't there. As my screams grew more desperate, the two women kicked up their heels and stepped over me as if I were a broken garbage bag leaking onto bleak cement pads.

As I slept in the unpleasant darkness, I could feel that I was being moved and shifted into strange places.

My eyes fluttered several times. I looked upwards to see many florescent lights. Too many of them stung my eyes and seemed to burn my skin. I was now dressed in a soft white shirt and white pants. The clothes were light like pyjamas.

"Are you awake?" A woman perhaps in her late twenties or early thirties stood over me. Dirty blonde hair was tied back in a neat loose ponytail. "I'm Doctor Noth. How are you feeling?"

"Sleepy. What happened to me?"

"Your father brought you here. You're here at Glemwood's mental rehabilitation hospital."

"Why am I at a mental hospital? How long have I been here?"

"Just since last night. You probably still feel funny because the sedative is wearing off. Now, can you take a deep breath and relax?"

"Can I see my dad?"

"Yes, he's here. Just a minute."

I rolled over and looked at my arm. It had a tiny bruise on it from the needle. Even the gentlest push on it made me wince.

"How are you doing?"

"Well, considering you sedated me, drove me four hours to Glemwood and locked me up with a bunch of other crazy people I'm doing real good, but right now all I want is to go home when can we leave."

"The thing is, Nikki, I want you to stay here just for a few days, maybe a week. You need a full recovery. I am not saying you're crazy. You're just under stress. Here you can relax and your nerves can too. If anything goes wrong, I'm going to be staying at a hotel just a couple of blocks away."

"Okay."

"Love you, Nikki."

Then there I was alone in a mental hospital, not at all the place I wanted to be. I wasn't really alone, though. Every hour Doctor Noth came in to check on me. And every meal a nurse usually came with a steaming bowl of creamy pasta and a Cesar salad with extra garlic croutons.

Since it was my first day (they made it sound like I was going to be here for a yearlong retreat), I got to relax for most of the day. After my last meal though I had to see the psychiatrist to talk about my "problems."

She turned out to be nothing like the image I had conjured. No boring hair or large black glasses. Her hair was shoulder length, shiny, and full of wavy black spirals. The outfit she was wearing was just as extraordinary: a short sleeved purple shirt. Short black skirt and fishnet stockings tight against her hairless obviously waxed legs. "Hello, Nicole. I'm Dr. Nikita. How can I help you?" She flashed me a perfect whitened smile.

I fiddled with a loose thread on the soft white pants as my story poured out. I have never seen a woman write so fast. Her pen moved as quick as lightning as she jotted down every single word of the story that I hardly believed myself. "Do you think I'm crazy?"

A thoughtful look spread across her face. "No, Nicole, I think you're under a lot of stress, though. Your file says here that you have no mother."

"Well, I used to until she was brutally murdered." I stopped after that, even though it had been ten years. The pain was still quite fresh.

"Do you prefer to stop?"

"No, my mom was murdered by two men named Kevin and Nicholas. They were never caught, and the police made me recite the rhyme."

"Do you mind telling me?"

Nicholas stood in front of me and blocked the view of my mother, and then he said:

"A-B-C one two three

She has to die, don't you cry

Slit her throat on this note

Blood come out, out about

She is dead all nice and red."

I hated that rhyme more than anything. What kind of sick bastard came up with that? Had they planned that or had he made it up? Sometimes I still heard his voice when I had nightmares. Lately, it was rare that I did not have nightmares.

"I see you have probably had these awful memories brought back, and since your father is working more hours lately, you feel alone and attacked. Your mind is creating a male presence, but because of your traumatizing past you have brought back the two men that murdered your mother."

"What about the letters?"

"I am positively sure that they are only mere fragments of the imagination. Well, of your imagination.

I nodded, but really I didn't feel sure that she was right. I knew what I had seen, and those letters were real. I had not imagined them.

"What am I going to do for a whole week here? How is this supposed to make anything better?"

"This is a very different environment for your stressed out body. Here we have excellent therapeutic rehabilitation such as spas, reading, and gourmet food catered to your liking. Since this area hardly ever gets snow, you can go for frequent walks around the grounds."

"Thank you, and you're sure everything is okay?"

"Positive. Now I'm certain that you would like to relax, maybe take a shower or bath if you prefer. Perhaps visit the library or maybe some of our other popular attractions."

"This sounds more like a vacation home than a mental hospital," I replied.

"We try to make our patients as comfortable as possible."

When I got back to my room, fresh clothes and a fresh made bed awaited my arrival. It must be nice to get special treatment like this, I thought happily to myself.

I gasped when I saw the bathroom. Light sky blue walls, white tiles, a large tub, and soft fluffy towels that felt like a combination of kitten fur and angora wool.

The water pressure was very powerful, and the tub filled quickly while I poured vanilla bubble bath in. It was warm and sweet smelling and very soothing. Even softer than my original clothes, the fresh white pair smelled of clean linen. They were light as bird's feathers against my skin. When I pushed aside the closet door, I revealed a terry robe. That even smelled like lavender.

My need for a pleasured reading grew. The library sounded best to fill my yearning. It turned out ready and able to fill not only mine but thousands of people's thirst.

Books were mounted on every wall. Shelves looked as if they bore a mass equal to a blue whale. There was every type of genre imaginable from fact to fiction, non-fiction, trivia, fantasy, sci-fi, horror thrillers, historical fiction and so many other titles that my eyes blurred when merely trying to observe them. I took a seat next to a very thin girl chewing nervously on one of her long light pale blonde braids. In her hands, she clutched several warm fresh-out-of-the-printer pieces of paper.

"Hello," she said without looking up. "I'm Tara. Are you new?"

"Yes, I'm under a tonne of stress, so now I'm here."

"I hope you feel better soon. I'm kind of in here for the same reason. My dad thinks I get a little too carried away. So he dragged me up here for a week and is staying across the street."

"Wow, we've both got a really similar story. What are you reading?"

"Some stuff I printed off about platypuses."

"Cool. Those guys are neat."

And then we just started talking. During the night I learned that Tara—that wasn't her real name. It was actually Trish—had joined the website BeTara.ca because many people bullied her at school. The website was based on some obscure celebrity and people trying to escape their problems by creating a more confident version of herself. Her identity was Tara star6. There she could be a whole new person. In many ways, she was a lot like me. She had no siblings, no mom, and lived with her dad, who was also in the military.

"What's your room number?" she asked snapping me out of my thoughts of our similarities.

"184."

"I'm 183. I wonder if they'd let us hang out."

I grinned holding the secret joke to myself. What a strange way to meet a new friend in a hospital. I hadn't had a friend of my own since my six-year-old days. "How old are you?"

"I'm sixteen."

"Me too. So do you want to go back to my room?"

"Sure," she replied placing her book back neatly on the shelf. The night went by fast. We talked for hours about anything and everything we could think of; we had so much in common. It was amazing. She lived in Sugartonne. She and I actually stood a chance of becoming close friends outside of this hospital.

At ten o'clock I went to bed and slept as peacefully as I had before everything strange had started occurring.

When I woke up a bowl of fruit salad, chocolate syrup, and a tall glass of grape juice rested on a tray at the bottom of my bed.

"Good morning, Nicole," a nurse with a name tag that read Cindy greeted me. "We wake all our guests at 9:15 promptly followed by breakfast. Enjoy and have a pleasant day, my dear."

The meal was delicious. Every piece of fruit—grapes, cantaloupe, honeydew, watermelon, and mango—was fantastically juicy and succulent

I couldn't believe being waited on like this for breakfast, three delicious meals a day, and a spa. This was truly amazing. A clean set of clothes was waiting at the end of my bed. Soft fresh linen: my favourite scent in the morning. It always woke me up in the morning and prepared me for the day that lay ahead.

Trish/Tara was waiting for me. She told me to simply call her T because both her real name and fake online name stared with the letter t.

Over the week we did everything together including the spa, therapy sessions, trips to the library, and for hours at night until curfew we talked about everything imaginable. But, when my week ended and our time to part came I cried, and thin tear streams dripped down my face as I gave her a farewell hug. We agreed to phone each other, but I never had the chance. A week later in the morning papers I saw her obituary. She had committed suicide. Life was truly horrible.

Chapter Five

Three Weeks Later

After getting home and grieving for my short-lived friendship, I recovered smoothly. How strange to be in a hospital because of nerves. Even though I kept telling myself that, a nagging part of me thought it was much more than that, far worse indeed. The story, the nightmares, the letters, everything that had happened to me was caused by someone with blue eyes or maybe it was green.

But it hadn't happened in three weeks; nothing had happened, not a thing. I knew it was bound to happen again, but I didn't want it to. I assumed if I just buried it away it would never come back. Sometimes that's the answer to things.

As usual, it was off to school, but I no longer had a long, painful walk since my ankle was now fully healed. "Bye, Dad."

"Goodbye, Nikki. Have a good day."

"I'll work on that."

I clutched my lunch bag and ran at a brisk speed. The wind blew warmly against my face as my feet pounded against the ground. It felt so nice to run again especially since I hadn't in such a long time.

It's funny that you do the simplest things every day and then for some reason one day you can't do them anymore, and you realize that you should really appreciate certain things in the world. I stopped at the door and walked once around the school to slow my heart rate down. Slowly the beating cooled to a more moderate pace, and I managed to walk into school breathing normally. As usual Miss Parker was sitting at her desk staring at her collection of papers. "Are you feeling all right?"

"Yes, much better." I hadn't had much school since I came out of the hospital. Only a couple of odd days where we scarcely did any lessons, but the hours today were more like a usual day where we studied history, math, science, language arts, music and then had gym. Since the school house had no room to act as a gymnasium, I ran laps outside and worked on improving my speed.

No mocking voice, no letters. Everything was as usual; everything was normal. As I sprinted back inside, Miss Parker was on her cell phone. She hardly ever talked on her cell phone at least not when I was around. "Nicole, I have something to tell you. I know this is very uncommon, but we will be getting two new students tomorrow, Evelyn and Natasha."

"They're moving here. Why?" I made no attempt to hide my surprise.

"Apparently their father is going to be trained by your father."

"I have been here since first grade, and suddenly its eleventh grade and we're getting new students. Why has it been so long?"

"Nicole, I know you're shocked, surprised, and probably a little nervous since you have been the only one here for a long time. But why don't you just head home and relax? It's nothing to worry about."

I nodded solemnly and picked up my books with no further complaints. I really didn't want her to be mad at me. If her temper flared, the following day would not only be miserable for me but two new girls because of my wrongdoing.

I supposed I should have been more excited and really happy; I had lived here for ten years and had no human friends what so ever. My company was the wildlife and nature. But even with these thoughts in my mind later at night I still tossed and turned waking up in cold sweats, my back soaked so badly I had to change my nightshirt. Why was I so worried? But just as I was almost asleep frightening whispers and horrific nightmares filled my subconscious.

"Nikki, are you okay? You were screaming." My dad shook me awake gently.

"Yes, what time is it?"

"It's 6:57. Would you like to sleep late?"

"No, I'll get up."

I normally got up around 7:30. About a half an hour earlier would not kill me. Then it struck me that today was not just an ordinary day. It was the day that new perfectly unusual strangers were coming.

I searched my dresser for anything nicer than what I usually wore. I had lavender skirts that I usually wore for a special occasion, but the dark skies loomed with the possibility of rain. We hardly ever got snow just rain. But the rain storms could get pretty heavy, and it would suck having to run home in a skirt. My wardrobe didn't offer many other choices, though. There were tee-shirts brown, beige, black and too many with army logos. I had sweats also in shades of brown, beige, black and classic grey ones. Or a pair of baggy camouflage pants. Other than that, I had a dingy pair of cargo pants that needed to be washed.

It didn't make sense though to get all dressed up. I hated dressing up. It made me feel uncomfortable and cramped. Besides I wanted them to like me for me, not some fake person I was not. In the end, I went with camouflage and a white army tee-shirt.

The walk to school seemed to take hours and the closer I got the school seemed to shrink, smaller and smaller as if I were a giant with a heart the size of a car that was going to explode.

But I did make it, and my large pounding heart did not explode. "Girls, this is Nicole," Miss Parker introduced me the minute my feet touched the school floor. "This is Evelyn and Natasha."

They were twins. They both had long midnight black hair that fell to their waist. Their faces were so pale, and their eyes were so dark they seemed like they were black. Natasha who sat on the right had a series of spirals, waves, gothic crosses, dragons and an endless set of black that curled around her neck and flew down her thin arms marked in the ink of a permanent tattoo. The tattoos were the only difference between them.

Ding, ding, ding. The high-pitched sound similar to a doorbell came from Miss Parker's cell phone. She picked it up hastily, her cheeks turning bright red in the process. "Girls, I have to go. I'll be right back."

As she left, I took my seat, and Evelyn offered me a sickly smile. "So your name's Nicole? Interesting. Have you been isolated in these miserable mountains your whole life?"

"No, I, well, we moved here when I was six."

"Who do you live with—mother or father? Oh right," she sneered. "I remember you now. Your mother's murder made news everywhere. Criminals never caught. You probably don't remember, Nat. You were away."

Natasha nodded. With tears in her eyes she handed Evelyn a note. "I saw it on the hospital television, and the nurses were talking about it."

"She can't talk."

"No, when she was six she got her throat slashed. They barely managed to save her. Nothing they could do though that would give her back the ability of speech. She's mute for eternity."

"How did her throat get slashed?" I felt uncomfortable with this entire conversation. Both of these girls were so strange, and their word choice was bizarre.

"How does anyone get their throat slashed? With a long silver knife that catches a shine in the moonlight," she replied bitterly.

Miss Parker walked back in at that moment. "Hi girls, are you enjoying yourselves?"

Natasha nodded, still silent. Her face indicated she was deep in thought. "So, Natasha, Evelyn, I have a few things to explain to you."

Almost all day she droned on and on making sure that they understood everything. They had gone to school in Calgary, a big city.

Never once had they lived this close to nature for sixteen entire whole years.

Natasha slipped me a note. "How have you lived here for almost all your life?"

Her sister mouthed the words, "bitch, wow, some new friends, yippee."

At lunch Miss Parker stopped for our break. I pulled out one of my usuals: a large bowl of mashed potatoes, with a side of chickpeas. I liked having hot lunches especially in the season of nothing but cold gloomy rain.

The two new students pulled out two blue bowls with three pieces of lettuce, finely diced cucumbers, and salad dressing so thick it looked like it contained no calories. They stared, and it was as if they hated me already, but what had I done to make them not like me? I stared back until they looked away turning to their stupid salads.

The rest of the day dragged on with no hope of an end. At 3:15 when we were finally dismissed. I had to hold down the urge to break out like a caged animal. As soon as I got out, the sneers vanished from their faces, and they followed close behind me like two little lost puppies.

"Nicole," Evelyn called out suddenly running to my side. "We live a few minutes away from you, but there are several turns we have to take to get there, and I don't want to get lost."

The truth was I knew all the marked trails on the mountain, and I knew exactly where they needed to go. The old fear cabin: three rooms all black and gloomy. It had been abandoned for years. But why should I help them? They made it clear it was not their intention to befriend me. I finally gave them the response they were looking/hoping for. "Yes, follow me."

"Thanks. Nat says thanks too."

After a straight trail past my house and two rights there we were at the old fear cabin, chipped wood, shingles, a cracked window. It looked the same mostly, but some efforts had been made to improve it. One window had been fixed, and some of the rotten boards from the stairs had been removed.

"Thanks so much. Would you like to come in?"

I nodded and sent a quick text to my dad. "Be home soon. Hanging out with the new girls."

The inside of the house was pitch black; I stumbled across a couple of boxes as we made our way to the kitchen. Nat gave me some tea while Evelyn fumbled blindly and aimlessly for something to eat.

Within minutes a china glass tea cup with a pink pattern and a plate of chocolate chip cookies were in front of me.

"So, Nicole, it's nice to have you over. Our father said it would be hard for us to make friends in an area so remote."

"I like it here."

Nat handed me another note which said, "Do you have any other friends?"

"No."

"Don't you get lonely?"

To almost all of her questions, I answered no. The darkness was so overwhelming that when I stepped outside even the almost hidden sun burned my vulnerable eyes. To my surprise, Dad was home waiting for me, his truck parked out back.

"Did you have fun?"

"The new kids are different, but I suppose they're sort of nice too."

"I worked with their father today. Kind of an odd man. He disappeared for hours at a time and barely did any of the exercises, and for the life of me I cannot remember his name. Something strange starting with an m."

For several more minutes, we made forgetful small talk and spoke about the new mountain residents when his face lit up like a Christmas tree. "I have a surprise for you. Do you remember your Aunt Denise?"

"Sort of." The last time I saw her was eight years ago at one of my birthdays when I still had birthday parties. The memory was fuzzy. All I could recall was a tall woman with dark hair.

"Well, since I'm away a lot I'd like to get something to protect you."

"Like an alarm system? What's that have to do with Aunt Denise?"

"Aunt Denise found a six-month-old seemingly purebred Bernese mountain dog. He's trained. He'll be your best friend and would fight to the death to protect you."

"That's amazing really."

"He'd be all yours." He slid a picture across the table. The dog had a black and brown patch covering both his eyes. His body was a mixture of shaggy brown-black and white fur. A patch of black looked like a saddle on his dark body. But my happiness vanished as I felt two freezing hands curl slowly around my neck.

I didn't dare speak. If I said anything or panicked, I'd be on a bus straight back to the mental hospital alone and unprotected.

"That would be awesome," I managed to choke. "When could we pick him up?"

"I don't see any reason why we couldn't drive down to Sugartonne tomorrow and get him. Yeah, you can have tomorrow off. We can stop for ice cream. My treat."

I nodded as if ice cream would fix everything. Things had not been okay in a while. Food would not come close to being a solution. Nothing could help me. I was going to die and end up being dragged to hell.

"Is something wrong, Nikki? You've still been out of sorts since your little trip."

By little trip, he meant the hospital. "Just overtired, that's all."

"Maybe you should go lie down. I'll straighten out your bed for you."

Chapter Six

I got into bed feeling like a zombie. I took a very deep breath, rubbed my blanket against my face and stared into my dad's deep eyes. It reminded me so much of my mother when she would tuck me into bed and sing to me sweetly until I would fall asleep.

"So, we're getting a dog tomorrow," I asked sleepily.

"Yes, you need a companion."

I nodded and just for a minute I wanted to close my eyes and lay my sleepy tired, scared, confused head down and just rest with no fear, worry, or problems. So much was wrong with my miserable life.

I dreamt of nothing. It felt nice and soothing to feel like an airhead, without a care in the world. When I reopened my eyes, Dad was gone from my room, and everything was dark. It was one in the morning. It felt like I had been asleep for a few seconds when it had really been hours.

My stomach growled like an angry bear, and I realized I was starving. When I went downstairs, to my delight and surprise there was a plate of chocolate chip cookies and a tall glass of soy milk on the table. This would be my second helping of cookies since I had eaten some at Nat and Evelyn's house, but I did not feel the need to set limitations on what I ate.

They tasted fantastic—gooey and sweet with a hint or maybe a pinch of salt. With the help of some milk the snack filled the emptiness in my stomach.

Dragging my feet, I trudged up the stairs back to my room. I found my computer screen flashing:

Kill Nicole
Let her burn in hell
He wants you
My fair maiden
Your blood
Your pain
Tears
Don't cry
But be afraid for in every shadow lurks a new evil

My legs failed me, and my knees buckled. I collapsed on the ground paralyzed with fear. They were only messages: white text on a black screen that made my pulse race. My heart pounded, and sweat dripped from my face. Somehow I mustered all my strength and barely climbed back into bed before the voices started. "Don't scream. I'm not going to kill you." A hand brushed gently across my forehead, and I found the voice strangely soothing. "I'll allow you to stay alive for eternity." And just before I was banished to the darkness, I saw a secretive hint of green eyes.

For the rest of the night, I wandered among the dreams that my vivid imagination had created until the light of morning opened the blackened cage I was trapped in. The window was open, and a cool breeze blew in. All I could think was that open windows let in demons.

A smile bloomed on my face when I realized today was the day we were getting a dog. I suppose I should have been more excited, but I felt like a walking zombie. The sleepless nights were taking their toll, and the nightmares were no help either.

Downstairs one of my favourite breakfasts was waiting for me—a bowl of fruit salad with grapes and mango filled all the way to the top.

"Your dog's waiting for you, Nikki."

"Hey, what's his name?"

"Twister."

I smiled and spooned some mango into my mouth. Twister was a nice name. From the picture it seemed to suit the floppy guy just fine. As usual, breakfast vanished just as fast as it was set out.

"Kaw." A raven's croak sent chills down my spine and made the mango taste like iron slicing my throat. A drop of fat blood dripped from the corner of my mouth. I reached for my napkin and hastily wiped it away. That only resulted in a red smear across my lips, which I licked off the best I could. "We have the eyes of the devil watching us," I said pointing to the raven's perch.

"Don't exaggerate. It's just a bird. You ready to go?" I nodded, rinsed out my bowl and left it in the sink to soak. Sugartonne, our destination, was about two hours away. A medium length drive down a bumpy mountain past about a thousand farmhouses that dotted the vast countryside.

But it turned out fine. I ate a bag of salted peanuts and drank a cream soda. After I finished my snack and had a short nap, we were there.

"You awake, sleepy?"

"Yes, sir."

We had stopped at a cluster of maybe twenty small houses all with golden numbers and cute doors. Out of house number five broke out a large dog and a tall, dark-haired woman. Twister and Aunt Denise.

"Hello, hello," she called struggling to get Twister to stop attacking a late season dandelion.

"Denise, it's so nice to see you." He shook her extended hand with his bone crushing grip.

"Hello, Nicole, it's nice to see you." She wrapped her arms around me gently kissing my cheek with lips as light as butterfly wings. "Could you please take Twister? He's making my arm ache."

Twister let out a defensive roof and promptly sat down by my ankles still snarling at the helpless dandelion. He was fairly sized. When he stood up he came up a bit past my knee.

Aunt Denise pulled my dad aside and spoke in a hushed tone. "I'm so sorry about this, but I don't think it would be a good idea for you to adopt Twister."

"Is there a problem?"

"Well, he's awful. He doesn't come when he's called, and he ate seven pairs of my underpants."

"He seems to be all right with Nicole."

While they spoke words that I barely heard, Twister rolled around on my lap. He had no response when I said his name. I had a theory about that, and that was he really did not look like a Twister at all. His eyes were gentle. I thought they said Marley.

"Marley," I said aloud, and he tilted his head happily. Yes, he liked it. "Marley, you're a good boy."

"Nikki, do you like him?"

"Yeah, he's awesome."

He shot Aunt Denise a warning look and motioned for her not to say anything. We were definitely taking him. "Do you have any supplies?"

She nodded. "I have a bowl, an extra leash, and some toys. He might want a bed though. I haven't been able to find a good one here."

"Well, we could drive to Glemwood."

I nodded and dragged Marley away from the dandelion. "Heel." He did as told. He was our dog, my dog.

Later that night I curled up in bed with Marley at my feet. Today was exhausting. We got Marley new everything. From toys to a leash harness and this awesome plaid dog bed.

He should be good for stuff for a while. No more trips to Glemwood, I hoped.

"Hnn," he whined scratching at my door as if he meant to say hurry or I'll pee on your floor. I hastily grabbed his harness and fastened the Velcro beneath his belly, hooked on his leash and attempted not to let him pull me out the door.

While he relieved himself on a nearby tree, I searched the darkness for something interesting to stare at. An eerie howl broke the silence, and Marley tried to howl back. "Come on before we get eaten by wolves." That was definitely not on my list for ways of dying. Being mauled by wolves would certainly not be favourable on my behalf.

He let out an unhappy snort and grunted with every second sounding more and more like a pig. After half walking, half dragging I managed to have him silently slipped inside before anyone was the wiser.

He circled his bed three times and curled up with his stuffed beaver. I made sure he was settled in before I went to bed. It wasn't long until he jumped up and lay on top of my feet. In one of the books I had purchased, it said not to let your dog sleep in the same bed with you because they will grow accustomed to it, and when they are full grown, you will have a big problem. I wouldn't mind. When he grew bigger I would just have to buy a bigger bed. My dad might have to loan me the money or buy it for me, but Marley was his idea in the first place, and I didn't think he would mind.

Chapter Seven

As I drifted off, I heard more howls growing nearer and nearer coming closer to my window until I saw a flash of black fur darker than night, and two eyes seemed to search for me in the blackness, eyes as cold as death.

I sat upright in bed wide awake and fully alert.

"Are you afraid of me, Nicole? Let me hear your voice."

"Who is this?"

"You don't know who I am, Nicole?"

"How do you know my name?"

"I know everything about you. I know what your intestines look like, and I don't even need to rip your stomach open with this knife."

Marley woke to bark in terror at the intruder. But the man was not alarmed; he simply raised his hand, and the barking stopped. Marley fell faintly, breathing lightly.

"What'd you do to him?"

"You need not worry, my fair maiden."

He stepped into the light so I could see him. His hair fell in dark, thick waves around his face and neck. His face was pale and ghostly white. He had the greenest eyes ever and was clothed all in black.

"Everything that's happened to you is my fault although some of the blame should be given to my cousin, anything involving death. His eyes are blue as ice, and if you see him, run for he will send you straight to the fires of hell, and you will burn in pain forever. Or he will send you to far worse places."

"Excuse me; I have to be dreaming."

"Not yet."

He raised his hand, and his touch stung my skin. The knife he had was raised high and was sent flying down into my flesh with such speed I couldn't even blink a searing pain. Suddenly, my whole arm began to throb.

"That was nothing," he sneered. "Watch this."

My blood soaked Marley's fur, and I screamed louder. Why couldn't my father hear me? He ran his hands over my back and felt my bare exposed skin that my nightgown did not cover. I shuddered inside and turned away. His eyes were fixed on me with such intensity I thought I would keel over.

"Sssssssss."

"What was that?" I cried jumping up.

"Watch and see, my fair maiden."

A large python with saliva laden fangs crawled over me, wrapped itself around my torso and began to squeeze. A low moan escaped my mouth as I attempted to crawl toward the man reaching out helplessly.

"Help me," I managed to choke, my voice very weak.

"Release her."

Slowly the serpent uncoiled and hissed at my ankles. I watched as it vanished. Pitifully I struggled to stand, but my legs felt as if they were made of steel.

"I'll wait for you." He knelt down beside me and gently lifted me, supporting both my legs and arms. He placed me back into bed and pulled the covers up over my trembling body. "Good night. Sleep pleasantly."

And as if by magic my eyes closed and I remained in oozy darkness until morning.

"Woof."

Marley woke me up barking. "Hey, bud." To my horror, there was blood on his fur. I attempted to wash it out, but a bit of saliva on my fingers would not do the trick. I reached for my water bottle, and my arm shook with excruciating pain. But as soon as I managed to stand up the pain suddenly vanished, and my pounding heart slowed to a normal beat.

For several seconds I just laid my head back and counted to twenty-five. Marley climbed on my lap and interrupted my silence. In a matter of seconds, two strong paws were pressed against my shoulders, and I fell backward as I tried to push him off.

"Come on, Mar. We've got school. Remember to be nice to Miss Parker or you'll get banned."

Even though I was acting as though I was fine, beneath everything I was traumatized enough to be locked in a mental hospital for the rest of my life. Still, I left for school same as always. Well, almost. This time I had a frisky Bernese mountain dog tagging along pulling on his harness and trying to maul acorns viciously.

As we neared the school building, I slipped a juicy red leathery skinned apple into the front pocket of his harness. It would easily fall out if he bumped it. That was the plan. The idea was for him to knock it out when I said go see her. We had worked on the trick all yesterday just using dog treats. He was really smart.

"Good morning, Nicole. Who's your little friend?"

"Marley. Go see her." I unclipped his leash. He ran up to her his whole tail wagging; all the while he licked her hand rapidly and affectionately. Before I even said the command the apple went thunk, hit the ground with a bounce and rolled under her desk. "What are you trying to be—teacher's pet?" She ruffled his fur. "I think it's working, bud." Without providing the poor damaged fruit anymore harm she placed it carefully on her desk behind her nameplate.

"Are Natasha and Evelyn coming today?"

"They should be here soon. Do you think they got lost? We have to keep in mind that they are new residents."

"I'll check on them. Marley, stay."

He dropped his haunches down and stared at Miss Parker mournfully, not happy that I was leaving. Sure enough, as soon as I opened the door, the two of them stood on the front steps with static hair and disorganized books that looked ready to fall.

"Sorry we're late. Family decorating crisis."

They slipped by me like two silent shadows and took their seats. "Why is there a dog in here?"

"That's Marley. He's my new dog," I said.

Natasha glared meanly in Marley's direction, and Evelyn shot me a narrow-eyed glance. Marley whined and licked their hands; it was obvious to me that he was just trying to be friendly and make their acquaintance. But they just grimaced and pulled away unhappily.

Miss Parker clapped her hands breaking the uncomfortable moment. "Natasha, Evelyn, you can both take a math and history textbook from the back, and we'll get started."

We worked constantly all morning starting with math and history, then moving on to science and some health. Finally, the time came to take Marley out. He had gone twice this morning, and once again he had to relieve himself on yet another tree. By the time he died there would be no trees left; he would have killed them all. "Come. We'll get in trouble because you have a tiny bladder."

For the rest of the day he slept, and we worked on an art project. I drew a willow tree surrounded by water. Its long leaves drooped and fell to the rippled water below them. It turned out much better than I had imagined. Normally I wasn't the artistic type. This picture, however, was not mine. Like the story it did not belong to me.

I was happy when the day came to its end. Voices whirred in my head, and I was the only one that could hear them. Wolves howled, ravens croaked, and so many eerie screams that belonged only in the fires of hell. There was so much in my head and no way to escape, no way to break free.

Marley tagged along at my heels lagging farther back when I wanted desperately to get home. But really what did it matter? Either way I was horrifically disturbed.

"He chained you down and said, 'Don't speak to me that way. You're breaking my heart.'"

"Who are you?" I turned in every direction, but I could not even catch a glimpse of the man from my nightmares.

"Of course, I can give you a name for even immortals have a name to address themselves with. My name is Twenty."

A number, I thought in disbelief. How on earth could a man have a number for a name? How had he made me so afraid and put my mind into confusion?

"How'd you do all of this? Where are you?"

Suddenly he appeared, and I saw him—the man with dark hair and eyes green as emeralds: the one that had cut open my arm and wrapped a snake around me. "I'm immortal. I am a Mecrathin, of course. You, Nicole, are a mortal human being, so you wouldn't know what that was. I am a demon, a ghost, and a vampire formed into one creature—a Mecrathin. And I want to possess your soul."

"Why do you want my soul?"

"Nicole, you are mine. I hope you understand because you will have to come to an acceptance of that fact for if you don't, you will be miserable for eternity."

I backed farther and farther away from him until I was up against a gnarled bumpy tree that shoved its rough bark into my tender skin. "What are you going to do?"

"Nothing, for now. Run along. Inhale the surrounding oxygen and enjoy."

He stepped aside as I dragged Marley away, running in fear. He smiled and in his smile two sharp curved back fangs became visible.

Marley whined because I pulled his harness, and it was now twisted awkwardly around his neck. He didn't seem at all concerned that this Twenty character was threatening me. No, that was fine with him.

"We've got to go. We have to get help from someone. No, no, no. No one will help us. We have to leave." I looked around frantically as if a magic portal would just appear and teleport me away from all my worries.

"Where ever you go I'll find you. You'll run and run and run. But eventually you will stop, and when you stop, I will be there. I'll find you always. You cannot escape me, Nicole."

I started to run again until I got to the house. I grabbed the door twisting it with all my strength. When it would not open, and my hands became too slick with sweat to hang on to the door knob I hit the wood as hard as possible until blood came to my fists.

"Your father is not home; you're locked out. Where are you going to go?"

That's when Marley finally seemed to notice the threat, and he started to growl viciously. His fur went up, and he showed all of his teeth. Twenty laughed and raised his hand once more. Marley fell to the ground. His eyes closed and his breathing slowed.

"What can I do to make you leave?"

"Nothing. I have to protect you."

"From what? You attacked me, and you want my soul probably, so you can kill me over and over. What can you possibly be protecting me from?"

"I don't want to kill you, but other people do. Immortals do too like my cousin Meraish. Remember when he strapped you down? He was imagining doing horrible, vulgar things to you, and he would act on those thoughts, and he would plan your death."

"Are you an angel of death? Are you from hell?"

"No, I am a Mecrathin from the shadowlands," he repeated this slowly and deliberately as if I were a small child who was incapable of understanding him.

"Dad," I screamed.

"He's not coming, Nicole. I guess we do have some time together after all, so maybe I can do something." Blood dripped from my hands and smeared on my pants. I was utterly defenceless. There was no on one to help me, nothing I could do.

"That's right," he said. "There is nothing you can do. So now just try to walk toward me. I'm sure you can do it."

Something came over me; something unlike anything I had ever felt before. A fear so strong I forgot even about Marley, and I ran as fast as I possibly could. And then as I was running the strongest force hit me full on like a freight train. Thick blackness overwhelmed me, and adrenaline coursed through my veins as I was thrust backward. The next thing I knew I was lying on the ground in front of Twenty, breathing heavily in fear and pain. He squatted down beside me and placed a cold hand against the back of my neck.

"Someone help me." I sobbed.

"Don't you just hate that, the feeling that there is nothing you can do, your weak defenceless powerless even? You'll feel that for eternity." My fingernails scraped the earth beneath me filling with blood and dirt; I couldn't stand or move. There was no way I could get up, no way to defend myself. Nothing.

Then there were footsteps, dead twigs breaking, leaves that had fallen and died being scattered. Someone was coming. "Help," I tried to scream, but it only came out as a barely audible whisper.

Twenty stood up and began to walk away. For a moment he turned back and looked at me with such amused cruelty I wanted to turn away, to block out his words, but I couldn't. "He'll be here for you later, but trust me. You do not want him to come anywhere near you now. Actually you probably never want him near you."

Chapter Eight

I was awake, away from Twenty and lying in my bedroom scared and alone. Well, not exactly alone. I still had Marley, but he appeared to be hypnotized and in some kind of coma or trance-like state.

And why did the date on my clock say Halloween when that was weeks away? Where was my dad? Why did I have hair that had suddenly grown to my waist and then fallen completely out and regrown to my crewcut length? Why did I hear screams? How was everything so messed up?

That's when the screams got louder, and I could make out a voice a young feminine voice, screaming pleas for her life, begging someone to stop. Was she with Twenty, maybe Meraish? Each minor second that I wasted her life was on the line. But why should I risk *my* life for a complete stranger? Or was it a stranger. Could it be Natasha or Evelyn?

Twenty had almost done something terrible to me, something horrible, and while he was taunting me, no one came to help me. Not one person in the entire mountain heard me. And what about in my nightmares? No one was there to help me then either. And here I was pulling on my shoes and grabbing a flashlight. I could hear her, and I needed to help her.

I ran down the stairs and shoved open the door. My flashlight gave me a little light. But the pleas grew louder and clearer. "Help me. My leg. It's caught in a bear trap. Help me, somebody."

"I'm coming."

"Help. It hurts. Wait. No, get away. No!" A shrill scream broke the air and the eerie stillness of the night. That's when I saw the blue eyes and the body of the girl vanished. This was Meraish; he was going to kill me.

I saw someone walking toward me, but it was not Meraish. It was the man from my nightmares—the African American man. His brown skin was scarred and dreads hung in his face. His narrow eyes were filled with cruelty. He looked strong as if he worked out. What was I going to do? Who was he? Was he the man Twenty said I didn't want near me? Should I even trust anything? Twenty said.

"Miss, I'm going to have to ask you to come with me. If you put up a struggle, I will have no choice but to be forceful with you."

"Excuse me." I didn't know what to say or do. Manners might be helpful at this point. Wasn't this struggle between me and the *Mecrathins?* Maybe he had made a mistake. Maybe he didn't know me at all. "I heard screams. I was trying to help. Do you know me?"

"Come with me," he repeated in a more serious tone. His voice was grim, and his eyes grew darker each step he took toward me. I saw he held a gun. My heart dropped. Was he going to kill me? Was I going to die? Twigs were breaking, and two glowing animal eyes appeared in the dark. A creature medium sized with blood on its teeth stood in the path.

"There is something out there," I stuttered inching my way slowly along the path away from the animal and the man back to my house.

"RRouuuuuf."

"Marley." I ran to him screaming his name. "Marley, help me attack."

A low rumble escaped his partly opened mouth, and he took a protective step in front of me. I had almost half forgotten about the man's gun until there was smoke, a pungent smell, and blood sprayed across me. "Marley."

He lay on the ground whining helplessly as blood leaked from his shoulder, soaking his fur and staining my hand. I ripped off my jacket and pressed it against his wound. Each second his breathing grew fainter. Even as I tried doing chest compressions over his heart and blowing into his mouth, his heart slowed. "Come on, bud," I wailed. "Stay with me. Come on. You're going to be okay. Come on. Keep breathing." His heart was barely beating now.

A pressure overcame my right arm, and I let go of Marley. I then realized I was still in grave danger with the man hovering over me attempting to drag me away. A needle pricked my upper arm, and things began to fade.

"Goodnight to Nicole."

When I woke up, everything on my body hurt, especially my pounding head. Where was I? When I tried to move, I found I was strapped down to a metal table. I tried to make out something, but everything looked like squishy blobs or collections of pixels that refused to stop moving.

With several deep breaths and five seconds of silvery darkness, I managed to at least look at my hands without them spinning out of control.

"Nick, she's waking up."

"I'll be there in a minute."

Two men came into view, and to my horror, I recognized them as Nicholas and Kevin. They looked exactly the same as they did the night they murdered my mother.

"Nicole, you are so beautiful. Kyle will be pleased," Nicholas said coldly as he ran his hands over my face. If I wasn't bound down, I would have kicked him. Unfortunately, I couldn't move at all. As his fingers neared my mouth, I bit down with all of my strength and managed to draw blood. "Get away from me."

"Well, well. You still are a little bitch now, aren't you?"

"What the hell do you want?"

"Our supplier brought us to you, and this plane we're on is going to make a little delivery. But I'm not telling you where we're taking you. I'm surprised my good friend Kyle wants you. I told him you were a piece of work."

"Nick, I've got the pills."

"Good, how about you shove them down her mouth?"

Kevin walked toward me holding several needles containing I had no idea what. "I have another idea. We'll use the liquid tranquilizers. Give me your wrists."

"I can't, you idiot."

He grabbed hold of my arm and prepared to shove the needle into my skin. "Hold still then."

I shook my head vigorously and screamed in his face. But that didn't stop him; he started to hit me over and over and then shoved multiple needles into random parts of my arms and torso. I hoped I would overdose. I became tired slowly, but I was still awake as they began to remove my clothes. I cringed because I did not want them to see me. They cut off my shirt and pants leaving me in only my underwear and bra.

Nicholas was the one to redress me. He took the restraints off my wrists and ankles. Then he had Kevin help me stand up as he slipped a long black dress over my head that was fitted with a tight corset. I remember being laid back down before I fell into sleep.

Chapter Nine

It felt as if seconds later someone was pacing around me anxiously checking my pulse.

"Kyle, she's fine."

"I really think you should show more concern. She is giving birth to your child."

"She's fine. The herbal drink was designed to knock her out for at least a week. That was plenty of time for you to have your way with her. That's what you wanted. Now you're sure she's pregnant. I'm not that much older than her. Are you sure she can do it?"

"Zelda, we discussed this before. You do not have the ability to carry a baby full term."

I was waking up slowly, but it felt so hard to open my eyes, and the bed beneath me was so soft I could easily fall back to sleep, but I wasn't safe. I didn't know where I was, and I remembered that I had left Marley. What if he was dead? Tears streamed down my face at the thought.

"Who are you?" I asked groggily.

"Oh, Nicole, you're awake. I was beginning to worry about you. You've been out for over a week now. How are you feeling? Well, we'll get to that in just a little bit of time. I would like to make introductions. First of all, I'm Kyle, and this is

Zelda. We'll have you up and walking soon. I know you are scared and confused, but we can't tell you where you are exactly, but you will soon be a member of this cult."

"Cult. What? I don't understand."

Zelda stepped forward. "Sweetheart, we are going to give you a better life. Here you will feel loved and accepted. No one will deny you what you need. First, you will have to have my baby."

"I'm not pregnant."

"Yes, you are," she replied pulling a match from her dress and giving light to a nearby lantern. "You are going to be the surrogate mother of my child."

She leaned against the wall with a pleased smile on her face, and for the first time I could make out their appearances. She had long hair as black as raven's feathers and a face more pale than chalk. Her lips were painted black, and she had kohl-rimmed eyes. I guessed she was in her early twenties.

I did not want to look at Kyle. He was a freakier version of Twenty. His hair hung to his shoulders and was as black as his gothic clothing. He wore black lipstick and also had kohl-rimmed eyes. When his eyes met mine, they shimmered nefariously. His skin was white as a sheet. Why was everyone so pale? Like Zelda, he appeared to be around the same age.

As I pondered how they looked, it hit me like a freight train. "How am I pregnant?"

"You've got to be at least sixteen. Haven't you had that talk with your daddy yet? You're a real woman now, and you're going to have a baby," Kyle said his voice low and menacing.

"No, no. Why?" I pulled on the cloth straps holding me down so hard ... Snap.

Kyle was quicker than I was. He grabbed me before I could get to the door and pulled me to the ground, pinned me down and stared straight into my eyes. "Doesn't that bother you that I know what you look like naked? And, well, I, let's just say it was fun."

"You sick bastard! Get away from me."

"Oh, Nicole, get used to it. I'll do it to you every single day. You'll like the sex."

"That's rape; you raped me. When they find me, they'll send your sorry ass to prison."

"They'll never find us. We can stay together forever."

He leaned down and shoved his lips against mine, pushed his tongue down my throat and ran his teeth against my face pretending to bite my neck. "Now wasn't that fun?" he whispered.

"Go to hell."

"Gladly. I'll take you with me. Now come, we have to get you settled in. The cabin will be your home for some time now. We don't like our pregnant women especially our surrogate mothers, wandering around."

"You just don't want me running away."

"That is true, but we'll fix that."

He dragged me out of the building and past small dark cabins and women who were holding young children. They saw me screaming and pulled their children inside. Oh, why bother to help me? Finally, we stopped at another smaller cabin, and he shoved me inside.

"I have a surprise for you."

I ignored him and continued banging on the locked door begging for help. He knelt beside me pushing aside the fabric of my skirt, locking a strange black device to my ankle.

I stopped screaming. "What the heck is that?"

He stood up and guided me away from the door. "If you leave this cabin a signal will be sent to this device, and you will be electrocuted. If you leave, you will be killed."

"What?"

"Exactly what I said, and you have a life inside you. Remember that. If you step out of this door, you will be a murderer."

"No," I sobbed. "I want my dad," A feeling of pure dread washed over me. "Is my dad dead?"

"No. What makes you think that? He's looking for you. Here watch this. They're talking about you on the news." He flicked on the TV.

"Hello," a reporter said looking very solemn. "This is Chloe Simonez for CNV News; tonight we continue the search for Nicole Aloevere. We have here tonight live Nicole's father, General Aloevere. Any words, sir?"

"Nikki, if you're still alive I will not stop looking for you. That's all I have to say."

"Now I have to go. I'll be back later. Remember, if you try to leave you will die, but I'll make sure you're tied just in case. I wouldn't want you to try and kill yourself."

He selected two thick white ropes and wrapped them tightly around my wrists and ankles leaving me stuck on the floor with no way to stand. I was too weak to put up a struggle. Whatever that herbal drink was it hadn't fully worn off and neither had the tranquilizers Kevin and Nicholas gave me. Perhaps they were also still in my system. I didn't even cringe when he kissed my forehead. "Nicole, you're accepting everything. Good, I'll be back soon. I know it will take some time, but this will become your home."

After he left, I collapsed from my sitting position and lay weakly on the floor. I wanted my dad and Marley. But I was almost certain Marley had died; he was bleeding so heavily. I wondered if my dad found him. When had he gotten home? When did he know I was gone? Why had this happened to me? Wasn't there a God watching over me?

Right now it sure didn't feel like it; it felt like I had been damned to hell with an embryo inside of me. I always imagined one day being a mother to my own child. But I had imagined being married happily and not being trapped in a cult. That wasn't too much to ask for, was it?

I was not going to keep this child. The child was Zelda's, not mine. Once with my dad, we watched this movie called *Surrogate*. It was about this female prostitute who was kidnapped, beaten, and raped by a very sinister man. She ended up being locked in the cellar of the man's house and became pregnant. When she gave birth to a baby girl, the man took the child and cut it in half with a butcher knife. That night the woman cried so hard she died, overwhelmed by the grief of her lost child.

I wondered miserably if that would happen to me. My child would be born, taken away and I would cry myself to death. I had no time to think of anything further because Kyle came back carrying a platter of something that smelled delicious. "I hope you're hungry because I cooked up something extra yummy for you."

Despite everything I was starving, but that made me angry because he had probably drugged the food so he could rape me later. "No thank you."

"I'll eat it. It's not poisoned or drugged." He lifted the silver lid and let the scent drift to my nose and make my mouth water, before popping a cube of dark meat into his mouth. "I have rare, well-done, and garlic spice. These are extra special meat cubes."

He untied the ropes and placed the tray on the coffee table in front of me. Hesitantly I reached out and selected a small well-done cube and chewed it slowly, expecting it to make me sick, but it didn't. It was absolutely delicious. I didn't eat much meat, but I was starving. It tasted just like the tenderloin of a steak with some Montreal steak spice. I took another one and then another. I guess I had been missing out.

"Is this steak? It's so good," I asked my mouth partly full.

"Oh, no. The animal it originally came from had two legs, not four," he said.

"So some kind of bird?"

"No, not a bird."

"What am I eating?" Blood dripped down my face as I chewed the last of the rare meat cube.

"You're eating a human."

"Oh my God!" I ran to the sink, my throat burning, and vomited every last piece of the meat up. Still, I had the blood on my teeth and my face, human blood.

"The meat shouldn't be bad. I killed her just this morning," he said.

Apparently, I hadn't gotten it all out. I threw up again, this time mostly bile and a bit of blood. I wondered if it was mine or the person's I just ate.

"Shhh, let it out." Kyle rubbed my back gently. "It's okay. Go and lie down. I'll make you some tea."

I stumbled over to the couch and collapsed. The couch was leather, and very hard; its armrest was not a comfortable pillow for my tired, sick head. He forced a glass of peppermint tea under my nose before I could drift off. How did he know I loved peppermint tea?

As hours went by the night took its toll, and everything darkened. Kyle wrapped his arms around me and picked me up as if I weighed no more than a feather. "Time for bed," he murmured softly.

The bed, unlike the couch, was very soft, king sized, five feather pillows, with a black comforter, velvety on the top, silky on the bottom, and an elaborate railing behind it that curved in gothic spirals.

"Are you feeling any better?"

"Yeah, the peppermint tea helped. Thank you. I'm really tired. I just want to go to sleep."

"You look beautiful when you're sleeping."

"How long was I asleep when I came here?"

"Just a little over a week."

"How?"

"Zelda, the woman you met today, is excellent at making drinks made of the natural herbs that we grow. If she wanted, she could put you into a coma."

I had a plan to distract him. All I had to do was keep him talking, and then when he was lost in thought I could knock him out and cut off the black device.

"So, Zelda cannot give birth."

"No, she can become pregnant, but the baby always dies before it's finished developing."

"I'm sorry to hear that."

He nodded, and there was a moment his face reflected an absent look. I started to inch away; I needed weapons—anything near me anything I could get my hands on, anything.

"Wait. Where are you going?" His head jerked up so fast I thought his neck would break. In seconds he grabbed my wrist and dragged me backward.

"Stop. You're hurting me."

"Where were you going?"

"Nowhere," I sobbed. "I needed a drink of water and..."

"You do not get up without my permission."

And one click and silver shine ended all chances of escaping. Now I was handcuffed. Great, more cuffs that dug into my skin the harder I pulled. The black device on my leg refused to budge no matter what I did; I was certain with all the racket that I was making Kyle would surely beat me. But he didn't. Several times during the night I would drift off but then awake screaming.

The third time I screamed so loud, and as I yanked on the handcuff I slit my wrist clear open. The wound stung badly, but I was desperate. At this point, I would cut my own hand off to get away. Even if I succeeded I still wouldn't be able to run. The minute I stepped out the door not only would my life be over but also the life of my innocent unborn child.

Still, wasn't I innocent? What had I done to deserve this? I wasn't alone for long. Soon Kyle was sitting beside me rubbing my back. "Nicole, you've done this three times. What causes your nightmares?"

"You do," I answered bitterly through gritted teeth. "You ruined my life, had my dog killed, and now because of you, my dad will look for me constantly. You ruined my life."

"You're with child, my dear. You're bringing life into this world. Doesn't this make you feel wonderful?"

"Not when my baby is going to be raised by freaks like you."

"After you give birth to this child, you can raise your own. You will learn to accept our lifestyle, and in time it will become yours too," he said.

I spat on his face and pulled harder on my poor, bloodied, handcuffed wrist.

"You're bleeding." His eyes widened, and a pleased smile crossed his face. "I must stop the bleeding." He un-cuffed me, but he held firm onto my arms.

"What are you doing?" I cried.

"You'll see. Don't worry."

He shoved my wrist to his mouth and sucked in the blood, then licked the skin till it was clean and the bleeding had reduced its flow. "I have gauze. I'll bandage it for you."

As he scrounged through his cabinets in search of a first aid kit, I wiped the saliva from my skin and continued my desperate search for weapons. No luck. It had grown darker, and I could barely see in front of me. I would need a map to find my hands. Everything was ruined.

Chapter Ten

The next day I was left alone, to read, clean, do whatever really. I was left untied; Kyle knew I didn't want to die. I searched every corner of the stupid cabin for some sort of weapon. But no, no knives, guns or anything even remotely sharp. Nothing I could use to injure or try to kill him. I couldn't even get my hands on a pointy stick to poke his eyes out.

So I spent the day cleaning every single nook and cranny until it was spotless. I just used water. I couldn't even find abrasive chemicals that would serve as a weapon. He would be thrilled; he would think in his sick little mind that I was adjusting. He could go to hell for all I cared.

It was not long that I was left alone, unfortunately. Kyle came back, his arms full of bags. "Hello there. Are you lonely yet?"

I shook my head and quickly scanned the bags. Nope, no knives or weapons. He was smart; he wasn't going to let me anywhere near a knife or his throat would be torn open. All the bags had were fruits and vegetables.

"You don't like humans. I assumed you might want to become a vegetarian since that's the only meat I can provide you; we only kill animals for protection, not for food."

"You kill humans."

"They're prostitutes. They have nothing to live for."

"Maybe they're just confused, scared, and mixed up trying to get money."

"You are quite the opinionated young woman, aren't you?" He leaned over and kissed my forehead gently caressing my cheeks. I smelled his aftershave and spearmint gum fresh on his breath. I wanted to pull away, but I couldn't. Something more powerful than me wanted him. "I can't do this. No please, stop." I ranted on like a drunken fool as he kissed my neck. I felt pin like pains race through my arm.

He placed a finger on my lips. "You need to relax; you have a new life. Everything in your past is exactly that—your past. It no longer belongs to you. You have to embrace this."

I opened my mouth to say something, but this time he kissed me, not hard or aggressively, not like he was going to rape me. It was soft and gentle. It made me feel weak and vulnerable. I was all alone now. I had only him. Was this love? Could he possibly love and care for me? He had taken me away from everything, made me pregnant and caused emotional scarring that may never heal. But there was something about him: his dark eyes, his gentle tones, and his warm lips pressed against mine.

"I'm so tired."

"You're drugged."

"What?" Now I realized the pin like pain had been a needle. He smiled almost kindly and laid me down on the hard couch. "You didn't sleep last night. You need your rest. You have to stay strong for the baby."

My eyes were so heavy they were hard to keep open. Things were beginning to spin as my vision blurred. But then I was on the bed underneath the blankets; he was beside me. He was touching me, his hand creeping up my skirt; his lips were locked with mine.

"No, stop," I struggled to say as he pulled away. I wanted to scream, but my voice was hoarse. I couldn't talk. I couldn't tell him I didn't want this. I wanted him to stop. He was hurting me; it hurt so badly. I tried to get up, but the medicine had now fully kicked in. It was too potent. He flipped me onto my back, and I tried to push him away, but he was just too strong. He kept hurting me, kept touching my skin, his hand like a claw; he put his lips to my neck. He was on top of me. I could feel him inside me, and it hurt. It was a pain that I could never have imagined. I felt sick. I could do absolutely nothing.

Then the blood came. He slit my wrists, drank from the wounds and cut my legs until more and more blood soaked the white bed. The wounds were horrifically painful; I was nearly screaming when he ran his fingers through them. Eventually, he stopped, and mercifully I fell into sleep.

As I slept, I dreamt of Marley. We were in a field of long, lush grass that brushed gently against my bare legs. We ran for what seemed like hours until we dropped from exhaustion. "I miss you." I sighed feeling lonelier than ever. I yearned for nothing more than to see him and my father again and be in their safe company. My dad always talked to me and made me feel safe; I always took his being there for granted. Now I wish I hadn't.

It seemed that I was transported to a magical sanctuary. Memories of my childhood flashed in front of me portrayed by colourful pictures.

My first loose tooth
Playing with little frogs
Mom holding my hand singing sweetly
Everything we'd do together

I missed the days when we lived in a large house with a garden and floors covered in plush white carpet. Mom would carpet clean them every Sunday. For carpets, it was like a world of soft.

The cabin we lived in was amazing also. It wasn't exactly a cabin. It was more like a small house, with a kitchen, multiple bathrooms and bedrooms, and even an upstairs. It would have truly been perfect if Mom could have lived with us. But she was murdered. It seemed so unfair. Didn't Kevin and Nicholas have family they loved and cared for? But that was actually why they killed my mother—for their own family, for their youngest brother, Luke. My dad told me one day what I already knew. He killed Luke because Luke was building a bomb in Afghanistan that was going to kill hundreds, maybe thousands, of innocent people. My mother was innocent; I was innocent. Why, if there are so many horrible people, why punish the innocent?

Chapter Eleven

Eight Months Later

I had slept for eight months. Not exactly sleeping; I was put almost in a sedated state. According to Kyle Zelda's magic little herbal concoctions were quite efficient when added weekly. I remembered being fed and taken to the bathroom, but it was all blurry. But Kyle said I was allowed to be awake for the last few weeks of my pregnancy. I was showing now, and I could feel my child's movement. As it kicked its feet and squirmed around, it was the most amazing feeling ever.

If Kyle had stopped checking on me, I would have been almost happy. He put me on bed rest, and the only time I was allowed to get up was to go to the bathroom. Then I would have to scream his name, and he'd have to remove the restraints on my hands and feet. He was worried I would try to strangle myself or somehow try to hurt the baby if I was allowed to move around. One, I would rather die than hurt my baby and two, I'd rather strangle him. I envisioned myself wrapping my fingers around his throat and squeezing his neck until his face turned blue and he dropped to the ground. I would never be able to do that though. He was too strong.

"How are you doing?" He appeared in the doorway silently as always, never giving me any warning.

"I'd be better if you'd leave me alone and take off these restraints."

He nodded, undoing the restraints first on my wrists and then my ankles. "I can't leave you alone though. You would get lonely."

"I'm not lonely. I can talk to the baby."

He smiled. "You will be a great mother to our children."

The idea of him raping me again made me feel physically ill. What could I do if he wanted more children? He was stronger than me, and he had his stupid needles filled with the awful drug that knocked me out.

For a few seconds of silence, we just stared at each other until a piercing scream broke the air and he ran to see what it was, leaving me once again to my solitude. I wondered if it was some poor girl like me screaming for help. But if it was I don't think Kyle would have reacted so strongly. Was someone hurt? Right now I couldn't focus on that because I was in pain myself. I had been having small stomach pains all morning, but this was worse. It was tempting to call him back. I really wasn't feeling that great.

My stomach ached increasingly, and I could feel the baby moving rapidly. Then, wet. Everything: my pyjama bottoms, the blanket, and the bed. My water broke. I was going into labour. "Kyle, help me. I need you, Kyle," I screamed as a severe contraction tore through my insides. "Get your ass in here."

I had never seen him move so fast. "You're in labour."

"Yes, I'm in labour now. Get me help you, idiot."

He dialled numbers rapidly on his cellphone "Get over here and bring the equipment." Without waiting for a response he hung up and was at my side.

"Breathe in and out."

"I'm breathing, you idiot." How many times did I have to call him an idiot? Why wouldn't he get me help? Pain tore through me so awful that I swore it would cut me in half; my screams could have shattered eardrums. But did he help me? No, he laughed mockingly.

My rage boiled over, and I punched his face as hard as I could. I heard his nose crack, and a thick stream of blood covered my hand.

"You bitch."

With one hand and my overgrown sharp nails, I grabbed his hair and pulled him to my face. " I don't care what I am. Get me help."

"Well, they're here."

The rest happened so fast I could barely blink.
Men came
Needles
Dizzy
Open stomach
Two baby girls
Zelda took the babies
Darkness
Stitches on my stomach
A basement
More needles

I attempted standing, but my legs were rubbery, and nothing on my body wanted to cooperate with me. Was I paralyzed? I honestly couldn't tell. The stitches on my stomach were torn, and the ground was soaked with blood. I lay on my back breathing heavily. Someone knelt beside me gently cleaning my wounds.

"Who are you?" I asked weakly.

"Shhh, it's all right. You've just given birth to two sweet little girls, identical twins. They have your blonde hair and hazel eyes."

"I don't remember. Its blurry."

"You're on heavy anesthesia. You had a caesarean section. That's why you're in so much pain."

"Who are you?"

"I can't tell you. I'd get in trouble. I'm going to get in trouble anyway, but I can't handle any more pain. I feel so much pain with this horrible ring in my neck."

I had noticed the strange metal piece in her neck with its circular end, but I mostly focused on her green eyes, which were the colour of olives. As she wiped the blood from my stitches her long, soft, dark hair brushed gently across my face.

"Please, can't you tell me your name?"

"Unfortunately, I believe it would lead to more trouble than it's worth. My master is very short tempered. Your master will be kind, though."

"I don't understand?"

"Twenty. I know he is planning to take you as his slave. I'm sure he will be good to you."

My heart was beating so hard I was worried it would suddenly stop. "Slave," I repeated.

"Oh, no. Oh my God, I'm sorry." She dropped to her hands and knees as a dark figure emerged from the shadowy corner of the room.

"I told you not to come here. She is not yours to trifle with."

I gasped in horror. The strange figure had no face. He was clothed in a long velvet hooded black robe. In place of his face were shadows, wispy black shadows that seemed to move like spirited tendrils of fog. He reached down and curled his long fingers with black nails into her arm, squeezing so hard that blood leaked from the small holes.

"No, don't take her away, please," I cried surprising myself as I managed to sit halfway up.

"Nicole, no, he'll hurt you."

He tossed the strange girl aside and took several steps toward me. "You are a worthless human, and you should learn to shut your mouth."

With that they disappeared. I wished the girl would come back. She was so beautiful. I enjoyed her gentle eyes and soothing voice.

For spending eight months asleep, I sure was tired, also scared, confused and lonely just to name a few. There was no bed in my dreary cell, just dirt and sharp rocks. From the appearance of the walls, I assumed I was locked in an underground cellar.

"Thunk, thunk." My head shot up at the sound of heavy footsteps, and a door that I hadn't noticed creaked open slowly.

"Nicole, so sorry for the poor accommodations. It's just that we have been awfully busy. There was a murder, and we were occupied with caring for the twins. Of course, they are with Zelda now." He reached down and helped me stand.

As he began to walk away, I grabbed his sleeve and forced him to stop. "Kyle, wait. Who died?"

"We don't know yet who it is. Our technical people are running samples of DNA through our systems."

As we walked back to the cabin, I thought of how everything was going wrong. The murder I could somewhat piece together. It was probably caused by Meraish. But who was the strange girl? Twenty not once, in the many times we had met, had mentioned any girl. I continued to follow Kyle silently and went to the couch holding my sore stomach. I was exhausted.

"Nicole." Kyle waved his hands in front of my face several times before I actually looked at him. Why did he have to always interrupt my thoughts? "I have something important to tell you. We're going to be attending a show in Paris."

My brain once again started to spin. Paris? What kind of show? Probably something sick and twisted from the depths of his warped mind. "What show?"

"You'll enjoy yourself."

"Why Paris?"

He sighed happily. "You've mothered two children, and I'm tired." He took my hand and pulled me up. "Paris is the city of lights. It is bright, extravagant, and you need to be around young women close to your age. These women are beneath you in values, but still. Plus your birthday is coming."

His babbling was always annoying, but it was true. I had completely forgotten my birthday, on August tenth. When you're kidnapped, drugged, raped and learn that some kind of Mecrathin creature wants you as his slave, you tend to forget about the day you were born.

"Tell me though. What kind of show is it?" I asked almost half curious.

"A show involving exotic dancers."

I gave him a disgusted look. "You're taking me to a strip club?"

"You can sum it up that way if you chose."

That made me so angry, and for the hundredth time, I wanted to scream.

Over the weeks that followed, I had to scoff at Kyle's idea of recovery. He drugged me up on weight loss pills after beating me for looking so fat. I ate little and worked like a dog. I packed clothes for us and cleaned the house from top to bottom. If I said anything snide, nasty, or sarcastic, he whipped my back. I did not mean figuratively either; I meant literally whipping me and dumping antiseptic on my wounds. Every night I curled up into a ball praying he would not touch me again, and late in the night overcome by exhaustion I would cry myself to a troubled sleep.

On the day we were to leave for Paris my morning, to say the very least, was hectic. I woke up at the early hour of three, finished all of the last minute packing, cleaning, and I phoned the list of required cult members to let them know that we were *splendidly* jetting off to Paris and would arrive home in several days. You would think any normal person would be unhappy at being woken up at three in the morning, but no. They all sounded as if they had been up for hours.

Once Kyle had mentioned that some cult members only slept for a few hours each night. I guess he was not kidding. With him, it was really hard to tell. His expression was normally grim, and he seldom smiled. When he did smile it was cold and unpleasant.

After about two hours of running around like a decapitated chicken, it was time to cook Kyle's breakfast and then depart. If I hadn't been going to Paris with Kyle, the trip would have been exciting. I always fancied the famed city of lights to be beautiful.

"No, stay focused," I said aloud. Right now was not the time to be thinking of my escape. Now I had to focus on cooking the human steak to perfection. Apparently, it was fresh. He had gone to the prostitute farm last night and let his guillotine taste young blood. The first time I cooked for him I didn't pay attention, and the steak burned. He beat me until I passed out. He liked meat rare and bloody, not charred. The message stuck; if it wasn't bloody enough he would slit my wrists open, and use my blood as if it were a sauce for flavour.

I let the meat cook for a few minutes on each side, so it was only a little brown. I didn't want to be beaten. After it was finished, I put the special finishing touch on the plate. A few leaves of salted, dark green romaine lettuce, just to add a sort of gourmet feel to it all. Since everything was set, I had a bit of spare time to myself.

I walked slowly to the bathroom and carefully pulled off my shirt. I grimaced at the thing that I called my reflection. My back was covered in a gruesome array of crisscrossed scars and still bleeding cuts that had not healed. The weight loss pills I had taken were effective, but the result wasn't attractive. I hadn't lost inches, but my stomach seemed oddly sucked in. I felt misshapen and ugly. As I put my shirt back on tears of shame welled in my eyes.

"Are you ready?"

"Oh my God," I screamed, but when I turned around, it was only Kyle. Not Twenty, Meraish, or freaky shadow guy. "You startled me."

"Is my breakfast ready?"

"Yes." I was planning on being very careful today, no sarcasm or anything. My back was too sore to be whipped, but there was still the long flight to endure. We were flying on a private jet since Kyle couldn't afford to have me in an airport fraternizing with people who could possibly save me from the hellhole that was my life.

"I hardly slept last night," he said suddenly. "I was anxious."

I nodded. "I see."

"Yes, oh, would you like a piece? This steak is delicious, and you haven't eaten meat in weeks."

"No thank you."

He leaned close to me. I could feel the warmth of his skin and smell blood on his breath. "Still afraid to eat your own species?"

"I'm not a cannibal."

"They are worthless prostitutes."

"Aren't we going to be staying with women that are similar to prostitutes?"

"Well, we are, but we are also visiting an old friend of mine."

I sneered. "You have friends?" but as soon as the words left my mouth I knew I had slipped up and angered him.

"Get on the floor."

"No, please. I'm sorry."

"Get on the floor." He was yelling now, and his face was red. He seized my shoulder and shoved me down. Before I could blink the whip struck me and immediately sliced through my tender skin as if it were paper. His anger was short lived, and thankfully he only hit me once.

I winced in pain and meekly climbed to my feet. Blood was already running down my back. Each time he whipped me, it became more and more difficult not to scream.

"Hurry up. We're leaving shortly." He jerked me forward without a word of apology. "Do not insult me."

I nodded and continued with the work I had to do. I lugged the bags outside and tidied up the half eaten steak. By the time I was finished my shirt was soaked and clung to my skin.

My crying was pitiful, but I couldn't stop. Slowly I removed my clothes and stepped into the shower allowing a gentle stream of warm water to wash away the blood. Living with Kyle had almost made me a first aid expert, so I had no problem cleaning the wound and applying a soft cloth bandage.

As I stood in our room wearing only a towel I searched for something to wear. Kyle had provided me with few clothes that suited my taste. My wardrobe held corsets, skirts, and dresses that looked as if they had waltzed right out of the medieval era. But my tee-shirt and pants were covered in blood, so I couldn't exactly put those back on.

I slipped on one of the dresses that I had left unpacked. I honestly didn't mind that dress too much. It had long velvety sleeves that dropped down when they reached my wrist and a spider web pattern that covered the front. Since I knew Kyle was angry with me, I decided to impress him with the whole look. Kohl-rimmed eyes, painted black lips, skull earrings, and a spike collar that looked as if it was made of thorns.

"You look so beautiful." He wrapped me in a careful hug and softly kissed my neck. "I'm sorry for lashing out at you. Do you need me to bandage your back?"

"No. I did it myself."

"Well, you have to learn some way. I promise I will work on a more efficient way to teach you."

More efficient? What was that supposed to mean? Electric shock maybe. Was he going to fry me every time I said something nasty to him? I don't know what he expected. I would never love him; because of him Marley was dead, and I was never going to see my dad again. He had ruined my entire life.

But I pushed those thoughts aside and put on my best fake smile. "We have a long plane ride ahead of us. I guess we should head out."

"You don't."

"What?" If I didn't go to Paris, I would never be able to escape. We were in the middle of nowhere surrounded by thick woods that went on for miles. I wouldn't get anywhere.

"You'll be asleep. I've got a special drink just for you. By the time you wake up we will be in Paris."

I let out a relieved sigh. I was still going to Paris; everything was going to work out. He had removed the black device a long time ago so I could leave the cabin without ending my life. I suppose he had taken it off after I had given birth.

It was a bit of a walk to the plane, but thankfully it was already loaded, and we were all set to go. When we were settled safely inside the plane in the air, he handed me a small test tube filled with thick yellow-orange liquid.

"This is drinkable. It's very sweet and will put you to sleep right away."

"What's it made of?"

"Mostly mangoes and some medicines for sleep."

"Oh well, I like mangoes."

He passed the vial to me, and I swallowed the liquid slowly expecting it to burn my throat or have some sort of unpleasant effect. But it was delicious. I felt my eyes get heavy and as I leaned back, the thick tendrils of sleep pulled me into dreams.

In the dream I was with Marley. He lay on my lap, his eyes soft and sleepy as they gazed at me. As I ran my hands through his fur, I noticed a small piece of paper wrapped around his collar.

It read: If you are reading this message now Marley is not dead. He is alive and well.

I wanted to stay with him forever, like the time I had slept for eight months through my pregnancy. But back in the land of the living, I knew Kyle would want me to wake up. Slowly I opened my eyes. As I looked around I realized I was no longer on the airplane. I was lying on a king sized bed in a lavished room. Also, I was not wearing my black dress; I was wearing a tee-shirt and jeans. My makeup and jewellery were also gone.

Kyle was nowhere in sight, but sitting in the corner of the room reading a thick paperback novel was a man who could have been the male version of me. He was about Kyle's age, maybe in his twenties. But he bore no resemblance to Kyle. At first, I thought I was imagining it, but he really did look like me. Crewcut blonde hair, hazel eyes, lightly tanned skin. Even sitting down I could tell he was taller and more muscular than Kyle. A more accurate description of him may have been that he was a small version of my dad.

"Bonjour, Nicole."

"Hi, I speak English."

"I know. I'm just working on my French. How are you, my dear?"

"I'm fine."

"Excellent. I see you are, and must I say you are also looking particularly beautiful."

"Well, merci," I answered jokingly. For once I actually smiled without being forced.

"Kyle is one lucky man to have found such a sparkling gem. Where are my manners though? I am Noah. Pleased to meet you."

"You as well. So you are Kyle's friend?"

"Yes, we used to be very close. We talk every once and a while now."

"He kidnapped me and raped me," I said bitterly.

"What are you doing? Who said you could talk to him?" Kyle burst into the room filled with rage. "What have you been telling him?" He reached for his whip and tried to pull me from the bed.

I had never seen anyone move so fast in my life. Noah lunged forward and pushed Kyle with such force they both fell to the ground.

"Noah, what the hell are you doing?" Kyle's voice sounded shrill.

"Calm down."

They climbed to their feet, hastily brushing themselves off. "Kyle, may I speak to you outside?"

After the door clicked shut, Noah had to bite down hard to keep from screaming. "You told me Nicole was a drug addict who needed to be taken away from her drunken father. You told me you had her bodyguard shoot a rabid dog. What do you think—that I live in a bubble? I've seen the news. That is Nicole Aloevere. Her father is looking for her. She lived with him happily, and you took her away and killed her dog. You had no right!"

"Oh, look who's talking, Mister? I give all these worthless prostitutes lives as exotic dancers."

"What I do is perfectly legal. If I ever see you treat her like that, I will report you and take her home."

"I'm going to marry her."

"What?"

"Tomorrow morning on her birthday."

"Well, good luck, man."

I was beginning to feel pretty anxious. Since when did Kyle leave me alone? But old habits die hard and there he was.

"My love, you are so strong, so brave."

"I didn't mean to upset you," I said giving him a really fake smile.

His expression lightened. "Do you mean that?"

"Of course. I'm growing more and more attached to you each day." The next words I was about to say would kill me. "When we get back I think we should have our own children."

His face lit up like a Christmas tree on the morning of the holiday. "That would be an honour."

I didn't know what he would be so honoured about; he had already raped me and caused me severe pain in my most vulnerable moments. But nonetheless I had to keep going. "Kyle, what time is it?" My voice must have been as sweet as a melted chocolate bar, and on my behalf, it sounded real and genuine. The plan was falling into action: butter him up so he would let his guard down, and in the silence of the night sneak out onto the streets of Paris where I would definitely find help.

"It's almost seven."

I stepped down with as much grace as I could manage, offered Kyle a sexy smile and kissed his cheek. I knew he would try and kiss me back, but for once I had power over him, and he couldn't do anything to hurt me. "So when does this show you were telling me about start?"

"In about fifteen minutes. I thought it would be nice for you to participate."

"I guess we should start getting ready soon then."

He had regained his composure, but I was still dominating him. "I have a dress for you to wear. Oh, my dear Nicole, how do you look so beautiful?"

"I'm not trying. Are you trying to be handsome?" My plan was certainly to seduce him, but I didn't know where all this was coming from. Luckily he was practically eating out of my hand.

"You're certainly lively tonight."

He led me down the hall into a dressing room that was as large as my old bedroom and pulled out a beautiful black dress. It had thin lace straps and was made of very light silk. Surprisingly that was all it had to it. "Care to try it on?" His voice startled me.

"Yes."

To continue surprising me, he actually left me alone and gave me complete privacy by shutting the door. At first, I thought he had done this to lock me in, but no; the door was left unlocked, and I was free to go as I pleased with no Kyle in sight.

Since I had nowhere to go, and my escape was not going to occur until later tonight when Kyle was asleep, there was nothing else to do but to try on the dress. As I adjusted the wrinkled fabric at my waist, I found it looked even nicer on me. The silk was so black and elusive it seemed not even to be a colour. For once in my life, I looked graceful and mature.

"Nicole, everything will be starting soon. Can I come in?"

"I don't know. Can you?" I replied sarcastically. It was Noah.

"Well, may I have a sneak peek at you in this most sought out dress?"

"Yes, you may."

The door opened, and he looked as if someone had ripped all words from his throat. "You look magnificent" was all he could stammer.

"Thank you."

He wrapped his arms around my waist, and our eyes met. "You're nice," I said jokingly.

"You're nice too."

We leaned closer until our lips were inches from each other. His arms around me were warm and gentle. I closed my eyes expecting him to kiss me, but he pulled away. "Why'd you stop?"

"Nicole, you are a beautiful, seductive, and very powerful young woman. But Kyle longs for your heart. His affection is very strong. I cannot betray him."

"He whips me, Noah. He doesn't love me. He hates me."

"No, he doesn't hate you. It's very complicated." He ruffled my fuzzy head in an attempt to lighten the mood and make me laugh, which really did not work.

Why was I so happy around him? I barely knew him. Yet at that moment I needed him most. He was someone who had shown me the kindness I most desperately needed.

With one final attempt to rid the awkward moment I spoke: "What's this show like?"

"You wear fancy clothing and showcase your beauty; your part is the ghost of white trapped by death."

"Okay, then random."

"Enough with the comments. We have to go. You get to dance for a while, and then you perform. Then you're free," he said.

Noah led me down the halls and up a spiralled flight of stairs to a large official looking room. The lights were dimmed, but I could see the setup of tables, a glowing catwalk, and clusters of young half-dressed woman standing everywhere. The music was loud and blaring, interrupting my thoughts.

I found Kyle waiting at a farther table fiddling anxiously with a small black box. He caught sight of me and hastily tucked it away into his pocket. "You look lovely tonight. I thought this would be a wonderful opportunity for you."

"Thank you. You look quite handsome yourself." Actually he looked exactly opposite; his dress shirt was wrinkled, his hair was messy, and there were dark circles under his eyes.

"Kyle, are you okay?" My voice was soothing, and for an added measure I gently stroked his hair, twirling thick black strands around my fingers and letting them drop against his forehead.

"I've just got a lot on my mind. You should see Noah. He asked me if he could have the pleasure of dancing with you."

I nodded and curtsied, but he was so down he didn't even smile. This was good for me. He was weak and depressed, which meant he would be distracted. All the better for me to make my escape.

As I looked for Noah, I noticed everyone was dancing; in particular, one group of girls stood out to me at the centre of the group. I recognized two faces: Natasha and Evelyn.

Chapter Twelve

Evelyn caught sight of me, and in a flash, she grabbed her twin's hand, and they disappeared into the pulsing crowd. In minutes I was standing in a hallway at the end of the room. There they were talking. They probably thought they had lost me. As I crouched down to avoid being seen, I could just make out what they were saying.

"Listen, Nat, she knows we're here. We have to get her or Meraish is going to kill us. You can't even talk because of him. If he kills us, you know what's going to happen. This is all her fault—hers and Twenty's."

I peered around the corner, but I could no longer see them. All that was left was a piece of paper. Cautiously I walked toward it, step after step as if the ground I was standing on were very thin ice and one wrong footfall would send me falling to a watery grave. The paper said only two words, but it felt as if it were my death sentence. You're next.

Someone placed their hand on my shoulder, and I screamed so loud I thought the fragile shell that was holding me together would shatter into millions of irreparable pieces.

The young woman beside me looked alarmed. "I'm sorry to frighten you."

"Sorry, myself. I'm on edge."

"The show will be starting soon. I'm here to help you get ready. I'm Sloane, by the way." She wore a tight black mini dress and over that a black robe that fell into silky tatters that nearly touched the floor. She looked a little older than me but much more attractive. Her hair fell almost to her feet and was very dark; it complimented her light skin and eyes that were almost black.

"I'm Nicole."

"Yes, I know. Shall we get ready?"

She pulled me through a couple of doors and helped me change into an outfit that was virtually identical to hers except white. For the final touch, she gave me six-inch killer stilettos covered in little skulls.

I smiled gently trying to meet her eyes, eyes being the gateway to people's souls. "You did that pretty fast."

"I help new girls a lot."

"When do we start?"

"Right about now. Come on."

Her sharp nails pierced my skin, and I yelped in pain as she pulled me along back through the hallways and into a dimly lit room. Following behind her was not easy. The shoes pinched my feet and were impossible to walk in.

"Ready?"

"Wait, no, no. Not ready," I screeched in protest desperately trying to escape her death grip. There were some other girls with her now, and before I knew what was happening she was pushing me through the curtains onto the overly lit catwalk. "Play along," she hissed wrapping her arm around me and then walking ahead. I took several hesitant steps forward most likely looking like a drunken elephant. Sloane, on the other hand, looked great. Each step she took was poised and delicate.

As I stumbled, she reached over and slipped her arm through mine. "Keep walking. We're almost there."

Really, I had no idea how she could even see. My vision was blurred and watery; the shoes were hurting my feet. "Okay," she whispered. "We're at the end of the stage. Be careful of the stairs."

She managed to walk down perfectly fine. I, on the other hand, slipped on the last step. Luckily no one was behind us, or I may have ended up being stepped on. I looked to Sloane for help, but she was already standing in the centre of the room. "We hope you're enjoying yourselves. The ghosts have come from worlds beyond, so live tonight like it was your last night."

Everyone cheered as about ten former prostitutes, now exotic dancers, strutted from their corners and walked among the crowds barely clothed in their skimpy outfits.

"Could someone help me?" I moaned rather piteously. I was still stuck on the floor.

Kyle rushed to my side looking much neater and confident. He knelt down and extended his hand, which for once I accepted graciously. Even as I regained my balance, putting almost all of my body weight on my throbbing left ankle, he remained on one knee.

The music had quieted, and everyone was watching us. "Nicole, you are a beautiful young woman. You are excellent, kind, and so very sweet. Each day with you is a new treasure. I would be honoured to spend every single waking moment with you."

Uh-oh, I did not like where this was going. What could I do? Could I collapse or maybe make myself throw up? I was feeling pretty nauseous, and that would surely stop him in his tracks. But I didn't react fast enough. He was holding out the little black box he was fiddling with earlier. Everyone else was silent watching me more than him anxiously.

"Nicole, will you marry me?"

What could I say? If I dared to say no he would surely whip me until I bled to death. If I said yes would he just drag me away, lock me within the confining walls of the cult and rape me, forcing to bring forth his children? I had already brought two poor little girls into that hellhole. Could I really do that again? The words were sticking in my throat like molasses; I had to say yes. I could not take his anger. "I will."

The people around us gasped and applauded; smiles broke out everywhere, and people were cheering. I could barely make out the sounds. All I could hear was my heart pounding, harder and harder with each passing second. Were my lungs closing? They felt so small. It was difficult to breathe.

"You don't know how much this means to me. We will be happy forever," Kyle rambled on and on. All I wanted to do was curl up and die.

"Please, excuse me." I had slipped off my painful shoes, and before he could answer, I ran as fast as I could out of that room. As long as I was anywhere else besides in there with him, I would be happy.

Actually, I was positive that no place would make me happy. My home might have done the trick or maybe my school. Okay, I admit there were a few places. When I stopped, I found myself in a large room with several beds. Perhaps it was a guest room. Honestly I didn't care.

The stupid show, mango drinks, Noah and finally receiving a proposal—everything had caught up to me. It was all very overwhelming. With a tired sigh, I managed to pull my sleepy body into the nearest bed. It smelled like fresh air and a gentle breeze on a warm spring day. Fresh sheet day had always been my favourite, and it felt like these sheets had just had their day.

I closed my eyes just for a little while and let darkness surround me creating a velvety blanket that was so soothing I never wanted to see the light again.

When I woke up, I found I was no longer in the comfortable bed. I was handcuffed to this white wall. I recognized the back room of Kyle's jet. So much for escaping. I registered that my handcuffed wrist was cut and bleeding. It kind of hurt, but was I crying? I could have sworn I heard crying.

Then the obvious occurred to me. There were two other girls around me. One had long hazel brown hair that was matted and tangled. Her eyes shimmered with tears. While she was thin, that paled in comparison to her companion. The other girl's bones stuck out in sharp angles; her blonde hair was thin and dirty sloppily tied in a messy up-do. Her eyes were hollow and weak as if she was very sick.

They were both bound with thick white ropes and had a black gag shoved in their mouths. At least I was only handcuffed and had one free hand. It seemed they had just noticed me and were trying desperately to talk, but the effort was useless. I gently removed the gag and helped untie the complicated knots that bound them. "I'm Nicole. Can you tell me your names?" I was trying to stay calm. I desperately hoped they didn't catch the tremble in my voice.

They were both so distraught the only thing I could really do was listen to them as they let their pent up feelings break free. The anorexic blonde was Sarah, and the perfect brunette was Starr. They were sisters. To sum up what they told me: they lost their parents at age fifteen and ended up in some pretty sucky foster homes. They slipped through the cracks of the system and prostituted themselves just to get money to survive. They were homeless and alone. They could not even afford one of the dumpiest apartments in the worst area of town. That is how they met John. He provided them with everything: clothes, food, shelter and anything else they possibly could have wanted. This lasted for about two years.

The life wasn't as perfect as it seemed. When poor seventeen-year-old Starr got pregnant he turned his back on them leaving them to fend for themselves. When they were kicked out, Sarah developed an eating disorder that did not allow her to eat. When she tried to swallow even the smallest morsel of food, it came right back up. Without John, they couldn't afford anything yet alone a visit to a fancy specialist for Sarah.

"Where are we going?" Starr asked wearily.

"I don't really know where. I call it the cult. Everyone does, even Kyle."

At the mention of his name the colour drained from their faces.

Starr tried to smile. "We were back to hooking when we meet this guy. He is so nice. He takes us out for dinner, and when he learns about Sarah, he says he can help us. We got to talking, and well, we told him what we told you. As we were leaving the restaurant, he holds a knife to Sarah and tells us if we don't shut up and do what he says he'll kill us. He gives us something to drink, and when we wake up, we're in this room. The things he did. He made us bathe in bleach. He took our clothes and," her voice caught in her throat with a choked sob.

That's when I realized they were wearing thin white robes; their legs and arms had visible chemical burns. Black bruises flowed beneath their skin.

"He hurt me too. Took me away from my family and... I can't even say it. I see his face every night in these awful nightmares."

Sarah looked up at me. "Is he going to kill you too?"

The question startled me. "I've lived with Kyle for nine months, and I'm sure if I do what he wants he won't kill me."

"Well, he's going to kill us. He said he'd skin us alive and then saw off our heads with a steak knife, so we have time to think about how we've been God awful whores all our lives."

These girls were so desperate and so scared I wished I could tell them that things would be fine, but they weren't fools. If they were even suspected to be former prostitutes Kyle would surely do everything Sarah spoke of. He had no use for them. At this point, there was nothing I could do to comfort them.

"Nicole, are you all right?" That was Kyle. He opened the door without further warning. "Why are their gags removed? They're untied. Why?" The veins in his forehead were bulging out; that's how angry he was.

"They were crying, and I thought they were in pain. I was just trying to help them."

"Do not touch them. Do not even look at them. Their vile touch will pollute your innocence."

My innocence, I thought bitterly. *If I'm so innocent why do you treat me so awful?* If I actually said that out loud, he would surely whip me, and that I could not bear. In a few moments of silence, his expression softened along with his tone. "We're less than twelve minutes away from home. Would you like to sit up front with me, away from these vile creatures?"

I nodded reluctantly as he unlocked my handcuffs and practically dragged me away. For the rest of the plane ride, I fell in and out of a restless sleep. Each time I drifted off something woke me, usually Twenty's voice. "I'm coming for you, Nicole. You'd better run fast."

"Leave me alone," I muttered over and over, but he would not listen to me.

"You're going to be mine forever. I like your little escape plan for Paris, but you won't be able to do that when you're with me. I'll always be able to find you."

The efforts I was making to try to scream, cry, yell, or even whisper a plea for help were physically draining. Besides who would hear me? Kyle? He wasn't exactly one for helping me, and there didn't seem to be any helpful magical beings stalking me.

Twenty appeared within my dream. He ran knives over my skin and caressed my face. He told me to sleep and said everything was going to be okay. It felt as if I had lain there for hours on end until he leaned forward and whispered four words that made my blood run cold: "I want your soul."

When I opened my eyes, I was standing next to a metal chain link fence. Sarah and Starr were standing on the other side. "Oh Nicole, you have to help us."

I realized I was at the prostitute farm as Kyle called it. He had taken me there once, and I swore never to return to the place again. Dark shacks scattered across acres of land, and the metal fence confined them within. It was at least 30 feet high with barbed wire laced across the top. Young women struggled in the horrid conditions, often severely injured and deathly ill.

The whole thing reminded me of a concentration camp from the Holocaust.

What was I doing here, and would helping them even be possible? I remembered the time I had tried to save the girl screaming in the woods. That had landed me here. Would risking my life help these two? Even if we escaped the farm getting out of the cult itself would be much more difficult. Our chances were very slim with the odds against us. Finally, I answered their cries. "We will have to move very fast, and you must understand if they catch us they'll kill us. But if you stay here you will most certainly die."

I grabbed the spare key taped beneath a rock, and as my hands shook, I pulled the lock open. They followed after me as we moved as fast as we dared. It took my eyes a bit to adjust to the low levels of light, but soon I could see just fine. Clear vision didn't make me feel any better. Outside of the farm, hundreds of houses stood seemingly motionless, but if anyone saw us the consequences would be horrific.

Sarah stopped short with a sudden cry and dropped to the ground. This was not good. We were between two houses, and they both had lights on. I dropped down taking Starr. "What's wrong with her?"

"She's having a panic attack."

"We don't have time for this," I said bitterly. We grabbed both of her arms and managed to get her up and back to running. Just as I thought we weren't going to make it. We stood at the less daunting wooden fence that had a large enough space underneath to crawl under. Sarah and Starr went. First, they were at the edge of a very thick tree line. Just as I was about to crawl under, pain tore through my shoulder, and I fell to the ground. A black arrow had gone right through my skin.

Through the pain, I managed to scream. "Run. You have to get away."

Sarah looked toward me. "We can't leave you."

"Run," I screamed, my voice ragged and desperate. I heard heavy footsteps just as I saw them disappear into the trees.

Once again I found myself asking the same questions as two men stood over me. Who were they? What did they want? Why did it have to be me?

As my vision cleared, I could distinguish the faces through my tears: Kevin and Nicholas. I wondered what they were like in their ordinary lives. Were they this horrible? Why had I met them in such horrible circumstances? Was it possible they could be good people?

I tried half-heartedly to pull the arrow out, but my attempts left me moaning in agony. This seemed to amuse Nicholas greatly. He knelt down beside me. "My little brother's hobby actually came in handy for once. When we were boys, he became quite the archer—could shoot a bird out of the high sky."

"You're going to burn in hell," I said through gritted teeth.

"Well, if I'm going there I might as well do this." He curled his fingers around the arrow and shoved the piercing point deeper into my shoulder and into the ground. I bawled screaming for anyone. I was in a position exactly like my mother was the night they murdered her.

"Your father killed our brother. So we took his wife. Now we are going to take you; we'll make sure he gets your body."

I now knew the whole story about Luke. He was going to blow up an Afghan school, and just as he was about to activate the bomb that would have killed so many my father shot him. "He saved lives. You two do nothing but cause misery. Why did you bring me here? Why didn't you just kill me then?"

"Kyle was supposed to make your life a living hell. Instead we find out he's pampering you, with trips to Paris, a beautiful home, and gourmet food."

"Yes, life here is wonderful," I moaned sarcastically. I was in so much pain I couldn't stand it. "If you're going to kill me get it over with, you bastards."

Kevin sneered. "We deserve to have a little fun. We had a splendid time with your mother, and you got to watch. Now it's your turn to enjoy the experience."

Nicholas pulled out a long metal knife with rusted edges and a blood-tipped point. As it neared my throat, I could feel the heat of his face and smell peppermint gum on his breath. I braced myself for the pain, but it did not come.

Chapter Thirteen

"Kevin, Nicholas, drop your weapons, and step slowly toward me. If you obey willingly I will make your death instantaneous and painless."

I felt the blade drop as Nicholas walked away.

"Who are you?" Kevin asked positioning another arrow. His demeanour was slightly guarded, but his voice was relaxed. He didn't regard this person as a threat. I couldn't believe Twenty had shown up; perhaps he would help me.

"I'm the object of fear from your worst nightmares. Now fall to the ground." They shook their heads mockingly and did the exact opposite. Nicholas retrieved his knife and pushed it against my throat while Kevin proceeded to fire the arrow. I winced struggling to move the blade, which was nearing my skin. *Come on, Twenty. Help me, please.* That's when they dropped flat on their backs.

When they were standing Twenty was shorter than they were, but now he was certainly in a dominating position. "You slit open an innocent woman's throat with a dull knife, so she felt it. Knives are fun to run along the arteries in the neck, but axes cut right to the punch, and they provide wonderful pain. You'll feel this."

He went to Nicholas, shoved the red blade of the axe deep into his throat, and then twisted it back and forth. That left him writing miserably with blood spilling from his mouth. Kevin was next. He screamed and begged, but in the end, the axe found itself embedded in his throat. Twenty flicked his fingers, and their bodies vanished.

"Nicole, it's so nice to see you again. That dress looks lovely on you."

I looked down and couldn't believe I was still wearing it; then the obvious hit me. "You saved my life. Thank you."

"Don't thank me yet. Your fiancé is coming. Don't worry though. I'll be back."

"Nicole, Sarah and Starr are gone. The bitches escaped on your watch." Kyle was suddenly standing over me. With each breath his face reddened more. This was an entirely new level of anger. "I was going to marry you and love you forever, but then you do something like this! Why would you destroy our future together?" He didn't seem to notice I was pinned to the ground with an arrow in my shoulder.

"They're gone, Kyle. They are going somewhere far away from this hellhole."

"You bitch. I don't need this in my life." He looked down for the first time realizing I was hurt badly. "What happened to you?"

Fuelled by adrenaline and pain, I ripped the arrow from my shoulder tip and all. Blood flowed down my side as I climbed back to my feet. I was going to bleed to death anyway; he could do what he wanted to—whip me, kill me. I was not going to lie down and take it like a dog.

"I thought you loved me," he stammered helplessly.

"Loved you? I hate you, you sick bastard! You raped me, and you ruined my life," I started shrieking, my voice a higher octave than I had ever heard.

His face was so red it was almost purple. He grabbed one of his needles and shoved it into my thigh. I stumbled, instantly feeling the effects. What the hell did he put in those? Just as he reached to strike me, his hand froze in midair.

"Kyle, Kyle, step away, and I'll spare your life. You can run back to your cabin and stay there locked within guilt."

"Who said that?" he screamed frantically searching the area for whomever had spoken to him. Just when he let his guard down, Twenty reappeared and forced a knife against the pulsing veins in his neck. This was the first time I had seen Kyle display fear.

Twenty forced Kyle forward with one hand, and with the other he dragged me behind him. "Well, well, the happy wedded couple. Who wants to have some fun?"

I assumed we were invisible because he had no problem dragging us between houses. Even the people who stood looking out their windows didn't see us.

"You're right, Nicole. We are not visible."

"How can you read my thoughts?" I asked skeptically.

"I'm magic. Do you care to know what Kyle is thinking? He is envisioning killing me and then raping you." He turned to face Kyle. "Good luck killing me."

Eventually, we stopped at a run-down shack. The wood that it was made of had rotted and was falling apart. I hated the shacks; they always reeked. As Twenty pushed open the door, the smell of rotting flesh hit me like a freight train. Two dead women lay in the corner, their arms curled over their bodies. They seemed so vulnerable in death.

He looked over at me and laughed as I tried to cover my face and block the smell. But quickly he turned his attention back to Kyle, whom he aggressively shoved against the wall, and curled his fingers around his throat. "You have lived a very sinful life—theft, murder, cannibalism. Look at all the horrendous things you did to Nicole."

He struggled to speak, but that was impossible with Twenty's hands wrapped tightly around his throat.

"Kyle, no one wants to hear what you have to say. It's time for your silence, so now you're going to be paralyzed just like this." He stretched his arms and legs out, so he looked like a human X. When he appeared satisfied he turned to me. "I am so very sorry for all the trouble this man has caused you."

Blood began to drip from Kyle's mouth and eyes in thick chunky streams. He had never looked so weak. That's when the knife appeared. Twenty ran it against his own face smiling cruelly. "The final step in emasculating you," he said and then shoved it straight into his victim's groin. His pained screams filled me with guilt.

"Nicole, it's time to leave. As for Kyle he will bleed to death soon."

"Wait, I know he's a bad person, but you can't just leave him to die like this."

"You still care for him. How sweet. Now come with me." He grasped my arm so tightly I could see black bruises forming beneath the skin.

Chapter Fourteen

Everything around me slowly started to blur until all I could see was black. When I opened my eyes, the room I was in was dark, and there seemed to be shadows of fog within the corners. The next thing I noticed was how cold the ground was beneath me. As I tried to push myself into a sitting position, I realized I was lying on cold, damp cobblestones. Last, I remembered the shack had a floor of grass. How had it changed to stone? Where was I? Where was Kyle or Twenty? Panic spread through my mind like a raging wildfire.

"Nicole, are you okay?" He squatted down beside me and gingerly wiped the blood away from my wounded shoulder, which I realized wasn't bleeding anymore.

"Where am I?"

"You are in the Shadow Lands in my castle." I didn't understand; my head hurt badly. He forced a cup to my slightly open lips. "If you even swallow a little it will make you feel significantly better."

I took a very small sip and swallowed nervously. It tasted pretty good like milk and warm, sweet honey. Within seconds I felt soothed and calm. That's when an eerie howl broke the silence, and I jumped to my feet.

"What was that?"

"My wolf. He likes fair maidens such as yourself. He craves their blood."

With a twist of his wrist, I was standing in a dark forest watching two glowing eyes stare at me.

Twenty stood behind me. "Run," he whispered.

I kicked up my heels, tearing my clothes as I tore through the underbrush. My bare feet bled as I stepped upon thorns, but I had much larger concerns. A huge black wolf followed close behind me. The faster I ran, the faster it ran. I was already running out of breath. There was no way I could escape. I guess Twenty grew tired of watching me run because the root of a tree suddenly seemed to uproot itself, which sent me sprawling to the ground. I wiped the blood from my nose and hurriedly tried to scramble back to my feet.

I was too late. The canine leaped forward and stood in front growling viciously as if it were daring me to move. I raised my hand to shield my face, but the next thing I know it had grabbed my arm. Its teeth had sunk into my skin all the way to the bone. I wailed in agony and without thinking ripped my arm from its mouth. I turned and ran scarcely looking to see what lay in front of me.

That's when I felt an immense pressure against my shoulders, and I was shoved face down. My back was torn from the wolf's claws, and I was bleeding heavily. Before I could react, it had grabbed the back of my neck, and I could feel the pain burning like fire. Blood dripped from its shimmering white teeth and fell as it proceeded to drag me forward. I caught a glimpse of its eyes.

They were such a deep black similar to a bottomless pit, a bottomless pit that showed no remorse, no sympathy, and not an ounce of mercy. Each step was more painful than the last. The bones in my neck cracked back and forth causing unbearable sensations.

Finally, it dropped me outside of the castle entrance at Twenty's feet. "You ran. Interesting."

Seeing Twenty's pleased smile the wolf turned and ran back to the forest as it vanished into the trees. The forest itself seemed to fade until it was completely gone. The castle was now surrounded by grounds almost like a meadow; there were people in the distance. What stuck out was the fact that everything seemed to be black and white, the grass was grey, the sun's light was black, and the shadows loomed in thick tendrils of fog.

"Why are you doing this to me?"

"You are female, pure and delicate. Your blood is meant to grace the blades of my knives."

The grave words made my heart stop, and blood run cold, forever, eternal, always.

I belonged to Twenty, and now there was nothing I could do. For such a long time I had live with the illusion that he wasn't real and that everything was going to be okay. I had never really believed that this would happen.

"Come with me, Nicole."

"No," I said stubbornly. There was no way I could bring myself to try and stand. I was positive the wolf had broken my neck.

He knelt down beside me and gently probed the shifted bones; his touch had a rather pleasant effect, and the pain was gone in seconds. "Come with me," he repeated.

I had tried to pull away from him. With my neck healed my strength had returned, but all the strength in the world wouldn't have helped me. He teleported us to a small cobblestoned room, and suddenly I was lying on my back. My wrists and ankles were held down by strong half circles of metal. No matter how hard I struggled, there was no way I was going to break free. As he watched me cry he stated clearly that he was going to cut my flesh open with his three favourite knives. I was now wearing a bikini with plenty of exposure to cut me.

"Well, my dear Nicole, let's start with the serrated blade. I always thought this one looked a bit like a crinkled French fry with the serrated edges on both sides. As it meets your skin, it tears with ease, but slowly pieces of skin are cut one by one mutilating your insides. Then there is the flesh blade. It's very long and can reflect the scared gleam in your frightened eyes. It is one of the sharpest knives and can cut straight to the bone. And lastly is my favourite knife: the golden dagger. The entire blade is made of solid gold except for the hooked tip. It can cause the most dreadful pain imaginable." He finished his explanation and ran his freezing hand gently against my ribs feeling my bones. His touch made my spine tingle, and suddenly I was freezing even though I was sweating heavily.

He selected his first weapon—the serrated knife. My eyes bulged, and I thought my heart would explode. The knife sunk into my stomach and went straight through to the back of the table. Strands of flesh tore from within, and as he pulled the blade back up, he twirled these strands like they were spaghetti noodles. His hands twisted as he moved the knife to the side gliding it along my lungs. Pain raged through me as if I were being eaten alive from the inside out. Blood was flowing from my wounds like a red waterfall. How was I even still alive? Twenty picked up on the thought. "That drink I gave you earlier prevents you from dying. Well, this knife is getting a tad boring. How about we switch?"

The boring knife was still inside of me. Before I could beg him not to, he ripped the knife out spraying blood over both himself and me. "Stop, please," I wailed.

"Why? This is getting fun."

The next thing I knew a horrific pain tore through my upper shoulder and sped down my arm faster than lightning. The skin from my arm was gone. I watched as it fell to the floor along with much blood. He then put the knife beneath my knee and tore the ligaments. He reached into the wound and felt the bone with his hand. Burning sensations engulfed my entire knee as if it were melting from within.

He looked at me with what seemed like sympathy. "You're doing well. One more, and you can relax."

The cruel tip of the golden dagger tore through my throat as if my skin were as thin as paper. This pain was different; it felt almost gentle, smooth like waves washing upon the seashore. Tears continued to stream down my face, and I felt so humiliated. I was tired of being hurt and tired of showing my fear, my sadness, which only seemed to encourage these sickos.

On my side I had endured the three knives. I had survived. I tried to be positive. I couldn't give up hope, but I was feeling so emotionally weak I wished I were dead. He ran his hands over the wounds, and they healed just like that. The metal cuffs opened, and I was free to sit up. I swung my legs over the table and ran my hand over my head. Twenty stood there just watching me.

"Please don't," I asked tiredly.

"Don't what?"

"Stare at me. Kyle used to do that to me; he'd make me strip naked and just stare at me."

"I'm not Kyle. I'm not going to do that to you. Stand up for me. "As I climbed to my feet he had me turn so my back was to him, my scarred back. "I can make those scars vanish."

"You can?"

He snapped his fingers, and as I looked over my shoulders instead of seeing scar tissue or cuts that were still healing, I saw the smooth perfection of unflawed skin. Then as Twenty continued his works of magic, I found myself clothed in a soft white dress with a neckline that wasn't too low and loose sleeves. Overtop I wore a hooded black cloak lined with silk on the inside and velvet on the outside that fell all the way to my feet. "I need to know why I'm here and about this world."

He led me to a comfortable sitting room where he began to explain things. It took a while. In the Shadow Lands, there were other creatures besides Mecrathins; there were Bloodens that looked pretty much like humans but were a strange lot: somewhat vampire-like, ghost-like, immortal. There were sorceresses who were basically female wizards, and Shadow Figures or, as Twenty called them, Ghostly Sirens. I was going to be turned into a Leekeen that was not completely immortal and the closest being to humans.

There were many things I was going to have to adapt to. Twenty would torture me for the rest of my life, and that life was going to be eternal. I was going to live to live forever without ever aging a year, week, day or even a second. I would stay the same now and forever more.

"Remember, Nicole, you belong to me and are expected to do as I ask you. I have many things for you do."

I didn't want to know what he was thinking. With my luck it would be horrific. "May I lie down? I don't feel well."

"Yes, you may."

His castle was all in levels. There were bedrooms, endless corridors, torture chambers and many other confusing rooms. After nearly an hour of searching and dropping from exhaustion multiple times, I found the way to my bedroom. It was certainly mine because my name was written on the door.

The room was a gothic palace. There was a large canopy bed with an all-black bedspread, a pearly mirror resting on what was perhaps a table for writing, and a wardrobe that was ornately detailed.

"Is your room to your liking?"

I nearly jumped out of my skin at the sound of Twenty's voice. "How did you get in here?"

"Magic," he replied meeting my stunned gaze with a sadistic smile. "Now come with me."

"I don't want to go anywhere with you."

He vanished and reappeared behind me before I could move, wrapping his hands tightly around my neck.

"Stop," I wheezed. He was cutting off my airways. He wouldn't listen to me. The air wouldn't go to my lungs; the tightening pain in my chest was worsening. My attempts to pry away his fingers were failing. Just as I thought I was about to die, he let me fall to the ground.

"Will you come willingly now?"

I nodded meekly, but I couldn't stand up. My limbs were weak, and they refused to cooperate. "I can't stand," I whispered.

He squatted down beside me and ran his fingers over my face. "You're paralyzed. You won't be able to get up." He took my arms and yanked me forward ripping open the skin in the process. "It won't matter. He'll sense you're injured and come faster."

He dragged me behind him, outside of the castle across the meadow and to this dreary wooden post, where he wrapped a frayed wooden rope around my throat. "You're outside of the castle alone and unprotected. Doesn't that make you feel wonderful?"

I pulled as hard as I possibly could on the stupid rope, but it had wire woven into its fabric, so all that did was slit my fingers open. Searing pain shot from my fingertips to my arms. I screamed and cried trying to get the rope off me. This only seemed to amuse Twenty. "Let me go."

"I can't do that. You're about to die."

"Die," I choked. This couldn't be happening. I was only seventeen and what about my dad? He would never find my body. He would have no closure for the rest of his life. That thought was more frightening than the possibility of death.

To my great displeasure he read my mind once again. "Just remember the drink," and then he vanished leaving me alone to wonder and cry. It had always been if I wasn't in significant pain I would try and hold back my tears. But this seemed like an acceptable time to just bawl. Choked sobs and pent up pain escaped my mouth as my body shook violently. I hated feeling so weak and idiotic.

"Oh, don't cry. Everything will be over soon, and you can sleep forever."

Even through my tears, I could make out a darkly dressed figure. "Twenty, go to hell."

"But I'm not Twenty. You know who I am." I saw his two blue eyes, cold as ice, first and then his pale skin and wavy blonde hair. "How could you not remember me, Nicole? I want you."

The word would not come, but now I recognized Meraish. It was certain. Now I had been abandoned and left to death.

"You're right, Nikki. I am going to kill you." He seemed to read my mind. I really wished they would stop doing that. I had so little things in my life, and now I didn't even have the secrecy of my own thoughts.

Eventually, I managed to gather enough courage to speak. "Why have you and Twenty done all this? Why me?"

"Because we want your soul. I will put you into a pleasant sleep where you can leave your pain behind and float in eternal paradise. I know you have endured much agony. Twenty wants to take you and torture you for eternity. Do you know where you are right now?"

"No."

"You're in a death lot. Some sick Mecrathins leave their chosen victims in these horrid places all alone to be ripped apart and, in most cases, die a slow horrible death. Are you hungry? Would you like to have something to eat— homemade bread perhaps?" A warm tray appeared, which he dropped at my feet.

I was so hungry I couldn't resist. I stretched the rope to its very end and shovelled the food into my mouth. Clumps of butter fell through my fingers as I chewed hungrily. Nothing had ever tasted so good.

That's when I remembered the story that I had written. I stood up very slowly. "You, you killed Winter."

"She was a useless piece of trash," he sneered his voice turning ugly.

"You started following me, and did you write those disturbing letters?"

"My victims wrote the suicide letters, and Twenty wrote some about you."

"Get away from me." I kicked at the post, tore at the rope and screamed as loud as I could.

"Leave me alone. I want to go home."

"Oh, Nikki."

"Don't call me that," I screamed.

He stepped toward me, and in a last attempt to defend myself I raked my hands down his face clawing his skin like a caged animal. He didn't even flinch though he just stood there staring at me. "I don't feel pain."

"Dear Meraish, you will."

His mouth opened, and he collapsed as a strange piece of metal stuck out through his neck. I was beginning to wonder if Twenty had come back. "He has a life ring in his neck now. It triggers the nerves and makes them especially sensitive to the slightest amounts of pain. This is what he deserves. Although he was going to kill you and send you to a place worse than hell." He smiled and stabbed Meraish in the back over and over. Meraish screamed and cried helplessly; he was coughing up blood. "Stand up, you fool," Twenty hissed.

His fingers scraped the ground beneath him, but he couldn't get up. He was in too much pain to stand. "I can't," Meraish moaned.

"Sure, you can. Why don't I help you?" Twenty reached down and yanked him up by his hair holding him up like he was a dog. "You kill girls. I know what you would have done to poor Nicole; you would have taken her back to your castle, and you would have raped her."

"You think you're better than me. I kill the bitches. They don't deserve to be alive. Strapping them down and cutting them open is so noble."

"You think raping a young girl, a twelve-year-old, is acceptable. Why don't you just try to seduce a woman and have consensual sex? Oh yes, it's because you're impotent. And if there were no females, you would have to rape young men, but you can't do that. Your magic isn't strong enough to subdue a male, and they would beat you into a bloody pulp." Seeing them standing there, they were both about the same height and built the same, but Twenty looked so much stronger, so frightening. I curled up in a ball trying to hide, but it was as if my eyes were glued to the scene. From the midst of the shadows, Twenty retrieved a small Exacto knife and shoved it into Meraish's heart. "You're barely worth that," he screamed as blood fell from his wounds. But in Twenty's eyes, he hadn't suffered enough. He soaked him in gasoline and then lit a very small match. "Time to say goodnight."

In a flash of purple and orange the flames engulfed his body, and then they seemed to glow black.

"Stop," I yelled trying to overpower the screams. "Why do you do this?"

"It's fun, my dear." He reached into the flames and pulled out the Exacto knife. His hand remained normal—no burns. He slit the rope and extended his hand to me. "Come now."

"I'm not going anywhere with you," I said stubbornly. I had seen enough of death and misery.

Once again he refused to listen to me and just teleported me back to the castle. I wrapped my face up in the fabric in my cloak and muffled a scream. "I demand to be taken home."

He pulled out his golden dagger and shoved it against my throat. "You will demand nothing." He tore the knife across my skin weaving the dagger's silver tip through the wounds path. The dagger vanished as soon as it had appeared, and the cut closed.

"That hurt," I sobbed.

"Do not demand things you will not receive."

"This isn't fair. Why me?"

"You're special," he said.

"What will happen to my dad?" I asked suddenly.

"His memories of you will slowly fade, and everyone else who knew you will forget you as well. It will be like you never existed."

I gasped, and an awful lump formed in my throat. "He's going to forget me." The tears flooded down my face.

He smiled sympathetically and stroked my wrist. "Nicole, I know this is a lot to adjust to."

"Leave me alone. You don't know how I feel!"

"Sad, upset, vulnerable, and a strong hatred toward me. I know you and your father were very close. He raised you, and look what an intelligent young woman you have become."

"He could have done better if he had had my mother's help, but Kevin and Nicholas killed her."

"And in return, I killed them and sent them to a place worse than hell."

I laughed and actually managed a weak smile. "What sort of a place is worse than hell?"

"Haven," he replied simply.

"Haven isn't a haven: a safe place like a sanctuary?"

"Not this Haven."

"What's so bad about it?"

"Haven is a place of psychological torture. You experience extreme thirst and hunger. Your worst fears are targeted, and you are faced with chaos. What is once hot turns to a frigid cold, the space beneath your feet turns to an abyss, and nothing is really ever there. And the Haven Keepers. You think I cause you pain. They live to hurt people. You can't imagine how excruciating it is being continually sliced open by their horrific scythes."

"I'm so tired."

He stepped closer to me, and I felt myself resting in his arms. "Can you carry me?" I asked plaintively.

"Carry you where?"

"To my bed."

"No."

"Come on, please. I'm being nice."

He looked at me and stroked my face, and the next thing I knew I was curled up beneath my soft covers. "Are you comfortable?"

"Yes, thank you."

"You're drugged."

"No, everyone drugs me. Not you too."

"You needed some rest, so the drink I gave you a few hours ago was designed to make you tired in several hours." It was amazing. I had been tortured and watched Meraish die. That had all happened in hours.

"You'll feel better in the morning. By then the drink will have worn off. Prepare to be in pain tomorrow."

"No, please."

"Go to sleep."

I reached out reluctantly and grabbed his wrist. "Don't hurt me. Please don't hurt me."

"You're mine now. I can do what I choose," he said calmly.

Chapter Fifteen

When I woke the blood from my wrist was flowing fast down my arm. Why was I bleeding? Why was I in so much pain? Why was I talking to myself?

"Are you awake?"

"I'm freezing." Once again I was wearing a stupid bikini, was in a lot of pain and didn't really know what was happening. That's when I realized instead of lying down on a table I was standing up with knives shoved through my wrists. "Please, let me go."

"You are going to stay here for eternity."

"Let me go."

"No."

"Yes."

"No."

"Yes."

"No."

"Come on, please. I won't tell anyone about you. I promise."

"You will never allow anyone to acquire knowledge about me because you are staying here forever."

"That's not fair. Why me?"

"We've already discussed this."

I twisted the knives against my wrist, but all that did was hurt more. I shifted the weight against the balls of my feet, which thankfully had no knives shoved through them, and tried to think of a way out of this predicament. "I wish I were a contortionist," I mumbled.

"And why do you wish that?"

"So I could kick these knives out, and run away, then curl up into a ball and then bite you if you got too close to me."

"I don't feel pain."

"You would if I bit you." I knew I sounded ridiculous, but I really didn't care.

"Well, my fair maiden, you would feel even worse if I sunk my fangs into your neck." As he smiled, I saw the two fangs within his smile. They curved backward into the depths of his mouth. As he leaned forward, I could smell spearmint on his breath. He put his hands on my shoulders.

And then it just happened before I could blink or do anything to stop it. I felt the skin on my neck tear open and the pressure of his fangs sink into the wound. The pain coursed through me like a poison attacking my bloodstream. My heart seemed excited tasting the sensation of the tainted blood.

His face was pressed against my neck. This was the closest he had ever been to me. Something distracted me—an awful, heartbreaking cry that echoed through the air. That's when I realized the noise was me screaming; it was so inhuman it sounded animalistic.

"Stop," I yelled. "Oh God, someone help me. He's going to kill me!" I felt every movement as he stepped back ripping his fangs out and tearing my neck in a jagged path.

"Why would I kill you?"

"Just get it over with, you son of a bitch."

He leaned in and whispered, "There's no fun in that."

"Somebody help me."

"Calm down. Put your right hand out."

"I can't. There's a knife in my wrist."

"No, there isn't." He was right; the knives had now vanished, and the wound on my neck had healed. Even though there was no more blood I felt sick and it hurt.

I looked down at my hands and then hid them behind my back. They were ice cold against my bare skin.

"Nicole, give me your hand."

I shook my head as tears fell into my open mouth. They tasted like ocean water. "No, please. I'm so tired. I want to go home."

"Nicole," he repeated patiently. His smile widened as I shook my head again. "Give me your hand." This time he didn't wait for an answer. Instead he just made my arm shoot forward with my fingers uncurled and flexed down at an awkward angle.

"What are you doing to me?"

"You'll see." Out of nowhere, a strange metal spike appeared. He ran his fingers over the sharp point, and it burst into flames. They died down into one black spark with a grey centre. It danced back and forth as if it were taunting me. "Perhaps you may want to look away." The heated tip of the metal sunk into my skin easily. Tiny sparks leaped from the fire to my hand and sent bits of melted flesh into my charred blood. After several minutes he finished whatever strange task he was trying to accomplish.

His objective became clear the minute I stole a glance at my skin. There was a tattoo branded into the skin of my palm: a plain black cross.

"You now belong entirely to me; you are a Leekeen. You shall live for all eternity."

"Forever."

"Would you like to get dressed? I'm sure you are uncomfortable. When you're finished come to your room. I have a gift for you."

"There is nothing you can give me."

"I can give you roses that are the colour of midnight. I could provide you with enough body oils you could drown in them. I can give you anything you can imagine."

Then he disappeared, and the outfit I had worn yesterday was folded up at my feet. Once again I was the gothic Red Riding Hood. I dressed slowly, finally slipping on my cloak. As I found my way to my room I hesitated to enter. So instead of pushing open the door, I walked in the opposite direction. Before long I found myself lost in a maze of corridors. As I walked, I noticed that I felt light, almost weightless. Was that because I was no longer a human? Welcome to my fantastic new life.

Twenty showed up as I was trying to decide which way to go. "I see you're continuing to stall."

"Leave me alone."

He took my hand and teleported us to what I was now referring to as my room. "My prison cell," I said bitterly.

"Hnnnh."

"What's that noise?"

"Hnnnh, hnnnh."

"What noise?"

"That noise."

"I suppose he's uncomfortable."

It was a dog whining, and I instantly recognized the high-pitched noise. Marley. In my haste, I shoved past Twenty and ripped the closet doors open.

"Marley, you're not dead!" I dropped down and wrapped my hands around him breathing in the gentle scent of his dog dander. "You saved him."

"He was in a pretty bad state when I found him, but with a little magic he healed up just fine. Now he can live with you forever."

"Thank you, thank you so much." I sobbed burying my face into the silk ruffles of Marley's fur. Even if I could never see my dad again, I had Marley. He was a piece of home.

"The man that shot him is now dead. One should not shoot someone's innocent dog."

The happiness brought back the memory of the beautiful girl that helped me after I'd had my twins. "Who was that girl? The one I saw when I was in the cult. She had helped me, and there was this man with her. He had no face. It was all shadows,"

"That girl is actually a Blooden. Her name is Raina, and the man with her was a shadow Mecrathin named Xephius."

"He was so mad," I said.

"Xephius is very short tempered. He did not want her to come and help you, but she left anyway."

"Wait, *how* do you know this?"

"Are you happy with Marley?" he asked distracting me.

"Oh yes, thank you so much. Despite the fact that you come off as callous you still manage to bring good into the world."

After Twenty had left, I climbed into bed and stretched out with Marley. "Do you not like it here?"

To my surprise he sighed and placed his head on my lap; his eyes were so mournful it made my heart break. I sighed. "Well, apparently I'm special, so now we have to live here. We'd better get used to it." I laid my tired head upon the soft fresh pillows. My pillow, my bed, all of it was mine. It was all my new life. On the positive side at least he was not keeping me in a dark and foul dungeon. It was so difficult to be positive in this place.

I wrapped my arms around Marley and sobbed. I swore the deeper I buried my face into his fur, the more I could smell of home, the pine trees, Dad's aftershave, the apple pie air spray that I sprayed in my room. Oh, how the scents were so comforting.

Chapter Sixteen

I crawled beneath the blankets and let myself rest. After a while, I must have dozed off because the next thing I knew Twenty was awake and talking to me. "Nicole, get dressed. We are going soon."

"Going where? I'm tired."

"And sad. Yes, I know. There is a clean dress hanging in the wardrobe."

"Where are we going?"

"We're going to get you a new playmate. Now hurry along and get dressed. If you're not ready in five minutes, I can always come and encourage you along with a little knife."

When I saw the dress Twenty had chosen, it wasn't anything close to what I had expected it to be. The top was in the shape of a black gothic corset while the bottom flowed out into tatters as if it had been torn up by a wild animal.

It fit very tightly, and I couldn't help feeling embarrassed, but really I couldn't do anything to protest. Marley looked up at me and whined. "I'm really sorry, bud, but you can't come."

"Nicole," Twenty called.

"Well, I guess it's time to go."

Stop one was the club and not just any club: the midnight hellhole one of the most advertised exclusive places ever, most notoriously known for its straight ice vodka. Twenty decided I could exercise control and obedience by wearing a certain collar made of barbed wire.

"No one can see this," he said as he tied it around my neck and pushed it into my skin. "If you step out of line this will be forced deeper and deeper into your neck until it sinks within your throat and sever your arteries. The internal bleeding is rather painful."

I nodded weakly, resisting the urge to scream. I wanted help so badly. When he laughed, I could see his fangs were visible. "And what would you like me to do?" I asked politely.

"Go and socialize with your former acquaintances."

"What?" I had no idea who he was talking about.

"There are two lovely young ladies that you know sitting right over there."

As I looked through the throngs of people I saw whom he was referring to me: "Natasha and Evelyn. No, not them. They want to kill me." I felt my collar tighten.

"Relax. You're immortal. Go have some fun." He pushed me forward, and I had no choice but to walk over to where they were sitting. "Hello," I said my voice barely above a whisper.

Evelyn smiled and pulled out a chair. "Nicole, what are you doing here?" Her voice was oozing with hatred.

I heard Twenty's voice in my head. Play nice.

I was about to sit down when I felt myself tripping over my dress. I tried to catch the edge of the table, but my fingers instead looped around a glass of vodka. As my hands hit the floor, the glass broke, and I felt my palms instantly bleeding. "That was an accident," I said stupidly as I stood up.

"No, it wasn't. I know Twenty made you do that. And I know he killed Meraish because of you. It is your fault."

"I don't know what you're talking about," I stammered nervously.

"Yes, you do, and don't play dumb, Nicole. It is very annoying. So what should we do with her, Nat?"

Nat shrugged and slid a piece of paper across the polished table. It said: "Kill her."

"Well, we can try, but it will be complicated and all with her being marked."

"Guys, please. You don't want to kill me."

Their eyes flashed nefariously, and I could see they held a demonic glow to them. They cocked their heads to one side, and it was if they could see straight into my soul. I tried to move or scream, really just to do anything. "Twenty, help me." My plea was barely audible.

They looped their arms through mine, and we walked daintily through the crowds. Several men whistled at us and waved. I could hear their vulgar thoughts burning in my ears.

Why wouldn't anyone help me? Couldn't they see I was crying and in obvious distress? No one came to my aid, though they may have been real nice people, and I was forced into a back room. Natasha pulled a wobbly wooden chair from the dust corner and sat me down. I tried to fight her, but they had the advantage of magic. In seconds my hands and feet were bound, and I was immobilized.

"What are you going to do me?"

"Kill you and send you to Haven where you can't cause any more trouble," Evelyn answered running her hands over my face.

"How did my life get so screwed up?" I mumbled to myself.

She pulled out a small thin bladed knife from the palm of her wispy hand and placed it against my throat. "Oh, Nicole, stop stalling." She cut a curved path from my eye down to my cheek. The blood looked as if I was crying. As real tears flooded into the wound, the pain intensified; if I had been standing I would have collapsed. She shoved the blade into my jaw and twisted it. I fought the urge to scream because I knew it would only bring her more pleasure. She leaned forward so that I could feel her icy breath on my face. "One little cut to your throat and you'll be dead. Don't worry. The Haven Keepers will take good care of you." She pushed her knife to my neck, and I could feel the skin tearing ever so slowly. She was certainly savouring this.

Twenty said I couldn't die, but these two witches were determined to kill me. Once again I was in death's hands. She was nearing the artery if Twenty was wrong I would certainly die soon.

But just at the last moment she stopped, and they dropped to their knees. Strange liquid dripped from their mouths, and they blinked their eyes rapidly.

"Acid is seeping from their stomachs and slowly burning them alive from the inside. They will be dead in a few hours, a day at most." I heard Twenty's voice in my mind, and then he appeared in front of me.

"Get me out of here," I hissed.

He placed the tip of his golden dagger against my throat allowing me to feel the coolness of the metal. After slitting my bindings, he helped me stand. "Those two are simpletons. They thought they could even attempt to kill you. Not with the powerful spells I have placed upon you."

"That hurt."

"Oh yes, sorry. I forget." He snapped his fingers, and the pain vanished immediately. "Feel better."

"Yes, thank you."

"You have one more thing left to do," he said.

"And what would that be?"

"You'll see. Just follow me."

"What about them?" I asked.

"Let the Shadow Figures die. Their only intention was to kill you. With a dead master, they will not be missed."

He led me back through the crowds, although I had a sort of false security with him, to another table.

"Nicole, meet John."

"Why, Nicole, you are even more beautiful than Stefan described you." He was in his early twenties and, in my opinion, very handsome. He had short spiky brown hair, rich blue eyes, and a perfect deep tan. I extended my arm to shake hands, but instead, he kissed my fingers. "It is a pleasure to meet you."

Twenty seized my hand and pulled me away. *What's wrong? I* thought.

He leaned in and whispered, "He's a rapist."

"What are you going to do?"

"Kill him."

"Why."

"Well, he is a horrible person, and he is going to kill several young women tonight. He just added you to the list."

"Why?"

"He thinks you're attractive."

"You know, I do actually take an interest in being involved in a conversation," John said irritated.

Twenty, who was posing as Stefan, wrapped his arm around me and guided me back to my seat. "Oh, don't worry. It's just a bit of sweet nothings between us."

"It's hard to find true love, but you don't need love to have pleasure. If she doesn't give it to you, you can easily take it. You look strong enough."

Twenty grimaced but didn't say anything; instead he changed the topic. "Would you like a drink? The blood shot is quite excellent. It is one of their finer vodkas."

Five minutes later we had three blood shots on our table. While ours remained untouched, John drank down his in a couple of minutes and ordered a second, then a third, followed by a fourth. When he looked away, Twenty added a little white packet of something to it. John, of course, didn't notice. He was too busy watching a skimpily dressed blonde bend down and pick up her wallet. When he went back to his drink, he swallowed a few sips and then put it down to rub his temples. "Well, this was nice meeting you, Stefan. Nicole, I believe you have my number."

"I do."

"I didn't give it to you. I must have gotten lost in those beautiful hazel eyes. He pressed a small card into my hand and smiled, although this time the smile was less perfect and more forced.

When he was definitely gone, Twenty turned to me. "He's going to die tonight."

"You're killing too many people. The routine is getting old."

"He was going to murder innocent women, and he wanted to hurt you too. Do you remember Sarah and Starr?"

"That was the John they told me about." I wanted to ask about Sarah and Starr—if they would be all right—but I was distracted by him removing the wire collar. "So is this it?"

"No, not quite. We still have one more stop to make. Do you remember Raina? She was the Blooden who helped you. I once owned her, and now I want her back. She was stolen by Xephius."

"What am I going to do?"

"Xephius is powerful. You get Raina out, and I'll show him never to take one of my fair maidens again. Use this knife. It's charmed."

I held the silver dagger close to me waiting for more directions, but the next thing I knew everything went black. Then I was standing in a dimly lit dungeon, and I could see Raina. Her features were distinctive: long raven black hair, pale creamy skin, and olive green eyes. "Well, call me your saviour. I'm here to get you out."

"How? I'm chained here. How did you get here?"

"Magic, at least I think." I set to work sawing away the metal that bound her. The knife sure did the trick because soon she was free.

"But why are you doing this?"

"Twenty wants you back."

At the mention of his name, a glimmer of hope crossed her face. "I've had so many masters. He was the least cruel to me."

"Well, he wants you back, so we better get out of here."

We heard voices yelling and then a loud bang. "What's that smell?" she asked scrunching up her nose. "Is something burning?"

"Oh my God, I think the castle is on fire."

"Bleee," a high pitch cry broke the air.

"Hershey," she screamed.

"What?"

"My goat, Xephius, tied him up in the lower dungeons. We have to find him, or he'll burn alive." She grabbed my hand and pulled me out of the cell.

"Raina, the whole corridor is burning. How are we going to get to him?" Fire had run up the walls and burned on the ground. Smoke was beginning to cloud the air.

"We have to get him. He's all I have."

I recognized the look of desperation and love on her face. I felt the same way about Marley; without him I was just a pathetic slave with nothing. She started to sob hopelessly. I had to help her. There were no other options. But just as we were about to turn and run, the fire engulfed the ceiling and one of the beams fell.

The rest seemed to happen in slow motion. I watched the beam fall and heard the scream. I saw fire run up Raina's leg. I helped her roll it out, and then we were limping down the hallway. She collapsed near a seat by a window where luckily there were no flames, and there was a slight breeze. I thought maybe she could just climb out the window, but one, it was barred, and two, this castle wasn't built by a dreary meadow. It was atop a cliff. We were so screwed.

"Bleee." The bleating of the helpless animal filled the air, and Raina began to scream.

"Nicole, we have to find him."

"Well, tell me how then."

"No, you have to let me help you."

"You're not going to be able to do any walking on that leg. Please, we're running out of time."

"He's in the lower dungeons. Just go down that staircase. He should be in the first cell."

Without another word I turned and ran down the treacherous stairs that were so narrow. I kept stumbling. I soon found myself in what Raina described as the lower dungeons. There were two wooden posts arched in a makeshift doorway.

"Bleee!"

Just as Raina had said, Hershey was in the first cell crying helplessly as the fires tore mercilessly through the castle. I pulled on the door, and when that failed I pushed against it. It wouldn't open no matter what I did. That's when I remembered the knife; I was still holding it.

The damp rotted wood cleaved in half as I stabbed it. I pulled the pieces of debris aside and ripped a large sliver from my bleeding hand.

"Oh my God," I gasped. Hershey's condition was beyond deplorable. He lay tied, covered in sticky blood. The floor was covered with carcasses of skinned animals, and the smell of decay was so strong I almost threw up.

"Bleee," he cried.

"Shhh, it's fine. Everything is going to be okay." I slit the rope and ever so carefully lifted him up holding him tightly against my chest. He was smaller than Marley and as light as a bundle of air. When I turned to the doorway my heart came close to stopping; I was staring into a wall of black fire. I turned away from the vicious flames and ran past the rows and rows of empty cells that had begun to burn. We made a right turn and came across two stairwells; the one that led up also led to the fire. We were left going down. Oh God, I hoped Raina was all right.

As we descended into the darkness, we found ourselves in a dead-end. These flames were spreading unnaturally fast. At that moment Hershey decided to break free from my grasp. He ran boldly back up the stairs bleating in triumph.

The fire had spread down the stairs and was coming closer to us. I managed to grab him by the scruff of the neck and pull him back to me. As I held him in my arms, the smoke thickened, and his body seemed to grow limper by the second. If he didn't get help soon, he was going to die.

"It's okay, bud. I just have to set you down." I wished that I was wearing a cloak so I would have something to make him more comfortable. As I lowered him down, he bleated softly and somehow tried to hang onto me. "No, you have to stay."

He blinked those watery black eyes, and I felt a sudden pang of guilt. This furry, little bleating goat was all Raina had. That made me work harder. I was attempting to break some kind of hole in the wall. Unfortunately, I had dropped my charmed knife, so all I was doing was shattering my grown out nails. I could feel the heat of the fire approaching. We were going to be burned to ashes.

Chapter Seventeen

Just as I thought we were dead and Twenty wasn't going to bail me out this time, we were suddenly teleported back to his castle. The first thing I saw was Raina curled up in a corner crying miserably. But seeing Hershey, she immediately perked up as he ran into her arms. "Oh, Nicole, you saved him. Thank you. Thank you."

Marley stood at the foot of the bed wagging his tail anxiously. I went to go to him, but that ever so painful voice stopped me dead in my tracks. "Are you all right?" Twenty extended his hand to me and pulled me up.

"Oh my gosh, I'm fine. What about you?" His one eye was filled with blood, and his shirt had been torn revealing a gaping wound in his ribs and shoulder. "Our plot is getting a little predictable, although I thought this might be the one time you didn't come for me."

"I told you I'd always be able to find you."

"What's going to happen to me?" Raina asked.

He smiled, and the sadistic edge that his voice was lacking returned. "You will live here alongside Nicole, and this time you will not be stolen from me. Now come along."

She got up and followed behind me leaving me alone with the little animals. I knew he would most likely torture her, but my thoughts were soon drawn away.

"Bleee," Hershey cried as Marley roughly pinned him to the ground and bit his tiny beard.

"Marley," I yelled trying to sound firm, but I was laughing too hard to command the nutcase goons. For the first time since I rescued little Hershey, I got to see what he looked like. His short brown fur was now shiny and clean. He was completely brown except for a white patch over his eye. "Come on, guys. Lay down." They dropped to the ground and stared expectantly at me. "Come on. Let's lie down." They obediently followed me and jumped up onto the bed.

I guess I must have dozed off because the next thing I knew Raina was sitting beside me stroking Hershey, and Marley was growling suspiciously.

"Cut it out, you. Raina's our friend."

"I'm sorry to wake you."

"Oh, no. No problem. It was just a catnap really. I pushed the blankets off of me and moved over, so she had some more room to sit comfortably.

"My hand hurts so much."

I noticed the same black cross on her palm. "We're twins." I held up my hand.

"This reality sucks. I mean, at one point you had a real life, and you were happy. I've been stuck here all my life. Oh God, I'm sorry that sounded so selfish."

"No, it doesn't. It's nice to have a normal conversation."

"It's just, why us? What did we do to deserve all this? Aren't we innocent?"

Innocent; the word seemed like a joke repeated over and over mingled with cruelty. Did I even know innocence anymore? The one thing I did know was "We're tortured innocence."

Three Months Later

The golden dagger with the tip of piercing silver ripped through my flesh at speed so fast I barely blinked as it tore through my skin. But the pain wasn't so evident to me; a greater horror awaited me. I struggled to keep my eyes open and to focus on the pain, but suddenly it vanished.

I closed my eyes hard. That usually helped me to wake up, but when I peered through my lashes, I wasn't staring at a cobblestone wall. I was looking at the brown walls of Kyle's cabin. My hands and feet were bound with thick white ropes. That's when two faces appeared—Kyle and Meraish.

"Oh, Nikki, you are so beautiful." Meraish leaned over me and pressed his lips against my mouth. His saliva tasted like blood. Kyle ran his hands over me; his vicious claw-like fingers groped my skin. That's when they started taking turns raping me. I could feel blood running down my legs as the heaviness of their bodies pressed against me. The pain of the assault attacked me internally and externally. I screamed as loud as I could, but what did it matter?

The next thing I knew I could feel metal, cool metal, pressed against my back and the metal cuffs over my wrists and ankles. I was wearing a skimpy black bikini. There were cuts on my legs and arms and deep welts in my bare shoulders. The wounds confirmed it; I was safe as safe could come. I was with Twenty. Twenty, the Mecrathin who had to save me from death and was kind enough never ever to rape me.

"You just fell asleep, didn't you?"

"Sort of."

The metal released me, and the blood vanished. I felt the security of cloth as I was covered with the white dress and black cloak. This had grown to be my favourite outfit: the gothic Red Riding Hood. I stretched out my muscles and let out a deep sigh.

He teleported us to one of the many lavish rooms of his castle, and I fell back into a comfortable red velvet sofa. He settled down in an ornately carved wooden chair. With a flick of his wrist tea appeared.

I took the frosted teacup gratefully smiling as the taste of peppermint danced across my tongue. "Thank you."

"Yes, peppermint tea—your favourite. Now tell me, how does one fall asleep when they are being tortured?"

"I can't sleep at night. The nightmares are terrible."

"And you just had one."

"Meraish and Kyle were there. They raped me. I keep seeing all these faces. Kyle, Meraish, Xephius."

"Xephius is dead; they are all dead."

"But what do I do?"

"There is a quote by Joseph Campbell: find a place inside where there's joy, and the joy will burn out the pain."

"And what if the pain keeps coming back all the time physical and emotional? Why am I telling you this? You cause me a lot of pain."

"Well, a prisoner doesn't usually confide to their warden. Go to Raina. She will understand your suffering."

"All right," I said reluctantly. My stomach hurt, and if I was sick, I wanted Twenty to be there so he could help me. With a twist of his wrist or a snap of his fingers I would feel better instantaneously. Oh, how had I adjusted to Twenty's cruelness in mere weeks? Raina hated Twenty. I knew that I should too. I was coping in my own strange way. Did I have Stockholm Syndrome?

I had no further time to ponder these thoughts before I was whisked away to another room. This room had dark red spiralled wallpaper, bookshelves filled with titles, and in the middle of the room, two rainbow coloured beanbags. Raina was sitting on the beanbag farthest to the right, but I noticed Hershey and Marley first. They were busily installed in their favourite pastime— wrestling. Marley had Hershey pinned to the ground and was moving in for the kill. He was attempting to bite his tiny beard.

Hershey's high pitch bleat broke through the air as Marley succeeded. Raina was keeled over laughing at the ridiculous sight. She tried to console Hershey while scolding Marley, but really she was laughing too hard.

I grinned to myself. Beautiful sweet Raina was very special to me. She risked her life to help me after I had endured my caesarean section. In the weeks that we had been living together, we had formed a bond that being torn in half couldn't sever. She had gone through so much, and even through her pain, we had helped each other cope. She and I plus our little animals. We were our own little family. In a way, Twenty even was a part of our union.

"Raina, what do you think of Twenty?" I asked settling myself into the beanbag.

She tried to avoid the question. "What do you think of Twenty?"

I played her game by answering. "It's really complicated. I like him and hate him. It's hard to admit it, but he is rather attractive and can be kind."

"Well, I feel a strong hatred toward him. Even though when I was with Xephius, all I wanted to do was be with Twenty. All the other Mecrathins treated me so mean. I'm just so confused, and everything is so freaking complicated. I hate life. I hate it so much."

"Raina it's okay, we're going to be fine. Just take a couple of deep breaths."

"I just really don't know how I feel about Twenty," she sobbed clenching her fists tightly and tearing at her hair. I grabbed her wrists forcefully to make her stop. It made my heart ache to see her do that.

"It's not easy living here. I have nightmares all the time."

"What about?"

"There is this one dream that I keep having over and over. I'm walking to school, and I see this huge hole. It has bars over the top, and the bottom is filled with rain water. There is this woman stuck down there, and she's begging me to help her. I turn and run because I don't know what to do. I see my house, and I think if I just run fast enough, I think I can get my dad to come and help me. When I get to the door though, Kyle's standing there. Then I turn away from him and feel his whip cut me. The next thing I know I'm wearing this black dress stuck in that hole screaming as the woman pulls me into the ground."

"That's awful."

"What about you? Ever have any nightmares?"

She shifts her weight and twirls a strand of hair around her finger. "It's weird."

"Tell me."

"Well, I'm walking into this room, and it's completely dark except for this stream of really pale light coming from an upper window. There's this little girl sitting on this rug brushing a doll's hair. I go over to her, and I realize that she is me. She reaches out to me and says it's time to play. I don't know why, but it has always freaked me out."

"That's certainly different."

"Do you remember last night?"

"I don't see how last night has anything do with this."

"Well, do you remember, though?"

"Yeah, Twenty took you away and tortured you. I know it's not overly nice, but I guess it didn't majorly concern me."

"He didn't though."

"He didn't?"

"No."

"Well, what happened?"

She paused. "It's complicated."

"Were you two talking?"

"No."

I was getting the sense she wasn't telling me something. "Raina, whatever happened you can tell me. I'm your friend. We're in this together." She looked up at me, and it felt as if those olive green eyes were latched onto my soul and trying to tear it from within me. "You can tell me," I repeated gently placing my hand atop of hers smiling the best I could.

"Nicole, I'm pregnant."

I suppose I could have tried to control my reaction. I leaped up running my hands over my head. "How the heck did you get pregnant? Did you, uh, do it with Twenty?"

Her eyes widened, and her cheeks flushed. "No."

"Then how did you get pregnant? You have to have sex, don't you?"

"No."

"I understood that sex talk with my father clearly enough. How else are babies formed?"

"There are other ways."

I took a deep breath and sat back down. "Do you mean like in vitro or artificial insemination?"

"Artificial what?"

"Oh, never mind. How did you get pregnant?"

"Even though you're a Leekeen you're still thinking like a human."

"I don't understand."

"A berry."

"A berry?"

"Yes."

"How do you get pregnant from a berry."

"You eat it."

"Okay."

"Well, this isn't just any berry. It's a vevlakaneeshnek berry, and they are incredibly rare. When you eat them, the seeds falls into your womb where it grows into a baby. Xephius said he wanted the baby to go to term delivered so he could rip it out from inside me."

"How far along are you?"

"Five months."

"Xephius sounds worse than Twenty."

"We've been through some messed up stuff," she uttered a tight laugh.

"Well, you got pregnant by a berry. I was raped by some idiot. He had me practically comatose my entire pregnancy. Woke me up in my eighth month, and I went into labour that day."

"Sick bastard," she murmured.

"After my C-section, I met you."

"I knew I needed to help you."

"How did you know about me, though?"

"The only nice thing that Xephius ever did for me was give me this mirror. It was magic, of course. I could watch people. One day I came across you. It killed me to watch what Kyle did to you."

"It was wonderful seeing your beautiful face."

"You're also beautiful."

I moved closer to her and wrapped my arm around her. "So do Bloodens ever get intimate with one another?"

"Bloodens don't usually have sex. There aren't male Bloodens."

"Do they ever explore other sexualities?" I couldn't believe I'd just said that. I clamped my hand over my mouth and blushed the colour of a ripe tomato. What a good way to wreck a friendship.

She didn't seem to mind. She cocked her head and leaned in close to my neck. "Sometimes," she said.

She ran my hands through her thick silky ribbons of hair. Ironically, she smelled like blood but also vanilla. She was so enticing, I could feel the energy flowing through her veins and into my skin. Then just like that, our lips met in a passionate, electric kiss. The only sexual experience I had ever had was with Kyle, which was not willingly or enjoyable. This, however, was different. It was like being drowned in caramel while lying atop of a cliff that you were about to fall off. Exhilarating and ever so sweet.

Chapter Eighteen

We pulled apart, and sort of just stared each other like two seventh graders parting after a school dance.

"That was nice," I said wanting to break the silence, but as the words floated in the air they sounded so stupid I wished I could snatch them back.

"I agree."

"Moments like that should never ever end."

She laughed and smiled. God, that smile was so beautiful. It made her eyes light up, and her face lighten entirely. "Aww, look at that."

In the corner of the room, Hershey and Marley were curled up together. Marley had his head over Hershey's back, and it seemed they were breathing in perfect harmony.

"Were you this scared?" Raina asked drawing my attention back to her.

I reached out my hand helping her stand and then pulling her close to me. "I was terrified because my girls were not only part of me, they also had Kyle within them. I was worried they would turn out like him. But your child was formed through a berry, so I am certain she will inherit all of your wonderful qualities."

"What if she acts like a berry?" she asked feigning horror.

"Um, I'm not sure exactly how berries act. I haven't been keeping up to date on the latest about berry behaviour."

She smiled as our lips met. I put my hand on her back, but instead of feeling the steadiness of her breath she felt as if she could barely stand. "Are you all right?"

"I don't know." Her voice was hoarse. She turned away clutching her stomach.

"Okay, what hurts?"

"I don't know," she sobbed. "My stomach. Oh, it hurts."

I wanted to say something about my pregnancy, how it hurt and how at times I felt terrible, but I would be lying since I had slept through all of my pregnancy. "Come on, maybe we can go for a walk," I said forcing myself to sound cheerful. I reached out my hand just as she collapsed. Her body crumpled as she met the ground; blood slowly leaked from her mouth. Hershey and Marley awoke from their slumber and ran to her. I did the only thing I could think of. Ran to Twenty.

Strangely enough, he was standing right in the hallway. "Well, well, my fair maiden. How are you tonight?"

"Raina's sick. You have to help her."

"Do I? And is that because you have found yourself falling in love with her? Honestly, I never pictured you as a lesbian."

"Please, Twenty."

"The magic words aren't magic here."

He grabbed my arm and proceeded to drag me away. He could teleport me anywhere he would have wished, but he liked the struggle. I fell to the ground trying to get back into that room, but he still wouldn't let me go. He held tightly to my wrist and dragged me through the hallways.

"You have to help her."

"I don't have to do anything." He smiled his usual sadistic smile. "That outfit is rather old fashioned. How about something a little more modern?" With a snap of his fingers I was wearing a tight black halter top and leather pants that fit like a second skin.

"Why are you doing this to me?"

"Because it's fun." He stood there curling and uncurling his fingers, watching me. His eyes were piercing: his sneer so sinister I could barely look at him. "Say, this is a chess game. It's your move."

I tried to run, but I found myself stumbling and falling straight through his body. That was an advantage of being part ghost. I tried to find him, but he was one step ahead of me reappearing not in front but behind me. "Checkmate." He grabbed my neck and thrust me against the wall, so I was now facing him. Resting in his hand was a rather imposing knife. Its blade was curved almost like waves and ended in a sharp glistening point that bent slightly down. "This is new. Just fashioned it last night actually."

I had nowhere to go. I was pressed up against the wall tasting my fear as it tried to surface. He raised the knife allowing me to catch my scared reflection before shoving its blade into my shoulder. Leaving me pinned against the wall.

My hands were untied, so I wrapped them around the blade's handle, slick with sweat, struggling to free myself.

"You're not going to get the knife out, not at the angle you're at. I know you injured that shoulder a few years ago. You were doing pull ups when you lost your grip. Of course, you held on with one hand and tore your poor shoulder from its socket. Your father helped you set it, but every once and awhile you feel the pain come alive. I can imagine how lovely this feels."

My left hand fell in resignation, but I couldn't bring myself to pull my right hand away.

"I don't know what you want."

"Blood and screams. You're in a lot of pain, but you're also a strong young woman."

"Screw you." He was correct about the pain. It felt like demons made of fire were burrowing through my skin.

He curled his fingers slowly around the blade's handle, eyes flickering as if he was challenging me. "How about we restart the game?"

"No, don't."

He pulled the knife forward maybe only an inch, but the pain was so excruciating this time I couldn't stop my screams. "There's the music I love to hear."

"What do you want from me?" I yelled.

He ran his fingers over my face. "I have to go now. My friend shall be here shortly."

He was walking away before I could stop him. What could he possibly be referring to? The floor was shaking, and I heard the cracking howls break through the air. "No," I wailed. Both the ground and the wall behind me crumbled, and I found myself falling for who knows how long. I felt air rushing up to meet me like speeding subway cars as my knees hit the ground and I twisted forward compressing my spine. I barely managed to raise my hands to protect myself from the falling debris.

Dust fell upon me as the last of the stones crashed to the ground, some crumbling into a series of chunks. Carefully, I traced my fingers around my shoulder. The knife was still there. Since it was no longer stuck in the wall I figured I could rip it out; it was just a matter of tolerating the pain. My fingers wrapped themselves one by one around the blade's handle. I gritted my teeth and closed my eyes. *Take a deep breath. It's just like ripping off a band-aid,* I thought, *only magnified by a thousand times.*

Something caught my attention, footsteps. Was Twenty returning, coming to gloat as I lay stuck down here? Did he want to see me rip out the knife? When I listened more carefully, I realized it wasn't Twenty. He didn't make the slightest sound when he walked. Whoever this was, their feet were clicking, like high heels. No, not high heels. They made a louder sound. Click, click, nails belonging to a dog. Marley, he wasn't that big. He didn't make such a noise when he walked. That meant, no, no. I refused to acknowledge the truth because it simply couldn't *be* true.

The shadow was cast over me, and I heard it jump down landing with ease on its four paws. The wolf.

Obviously, he remembered me fondly. As those dark eyes gazed straight through me I felt the minor fear pooling across my mind flood into full-fledged terror. I was screwed. That's when I remembered I had a weapon and a small chance to defend myself. Perhaps he was an ordinary wolf, and I could kill him; unlikely though. Mortals weren't common in the Shadow Lands, and death was only an outcome if you were very powerful like Twenty. Before I could panic and just curl up in a ball trying to hide, I ripped the knife out so suddenly I wasn't sure who was more surprised, the wolf or me. I attempted feebly to stab him, but he merely stepped aside, and I fell sending tremors of pain through my back. With remarkable speed, he grabbed my wrist, and as I tried to pull away, I realized how fully exposed my neck was. He must have too, but just as his fangs were about to tear into my throat, he stood up and walked away.

Perhaps Twenty had told him enough, or he simply grew bored. It didn't matter. I was in so much pain I simply lay there until somehow I found sleep.

I woke up in the middle to blood curling howls; I scrambled to my feet and ran without thought. If that wolf came back, he would certainly kill me. "Run fast, my fair maiden," Twenty's voice echoed through the catacombs of my mind. The thing was, I used to run all the time, and I was rather good at it, but I hadn't run in a long time. The efforts were draining. I stopped when I was nearly blinded by light—sunlight, natural sunlight, and the meadow. The grass was green: a beautiful green. Oh, and were those, yes, they were real actual people. As I neared the crowd, I saw him. Crewcut hair, tall, muscular and fit. My father.

"Dad," I called out. Oh my gosh, I couldn't believe it!

He didn't acknowledge me, though. Instead, he wrapped his arm around the woman beside him. I didn't recognize her at first until I registered her features: pasty pale complexion, frizzy black hair, and her ever so gentle blue eyes. They were both so dressed up, Dad in a suit, Mom in an elegant black dress. Why were they dressed like this? Why couldn't they hear me?

There were more people standing around them. Everyone was dressed in black; sorrowful expressions draped across their faces. I recognized these people as the soldiers my dad worked with, Mom's friends (the ones she went out for tea with). There were Miss Parker, Aunt Denise, and some of my cousins.

"Hello," I screamed.

"Let us pray," a man said his voice calming and soothing. Everyone listened to him, immediately folding their hands together. He looked like a priest. Was this, no, it couldn't be. I ran to the front even though I was still out of breath. There were pictures of me sitting on the couch looking like an idiot trying to pose like a model, hugging Marley, wearing my dad's military uniform that was far too big for me. The last one of me was when I was little, probably about five. I still had long hair, holding a frog in my hands.

Between the pictures was a smooth white coffin. This was my funeral.

"No," I shrieked, my hysteria rising. "I'm not dead."

Chapter Nineteen

I screamed until I woke up. I was still lying where I had fallen. I was still wearing the halter top and leather pants. The pain in my back had vanished, and my knees no longer felt like they were smashed. I felt my shoulder; I also found that that wound had closed. I was in perfect shape except for the wound on my ribs. Gosh, that hurt. Oh great, I had lain on that knife. I stood up, thinking I should just leave it there or maybe try to smash it into a million pieces. It would serve him right to leave me down here. On second thought though, I decide to take it with me. It would be nice to be on an equal plane with him. He always had a knife, of course. He could just make it vanish from my hand. I decided not to think about that.

I walked in the same direction I had in my dream. Instead of finding myself walking into a meadow I stood at the foot of the staircase. That reminded me of being in Xephius's castle; I guess , Twenty wasn't interested in watching me wander around so the next thing I knew I was standing in a torture chamber.

"Raina." She lay slightly curled up on that inhuman metal slab of a table. "You're not restrained. Can you get up?"

"No, I'm paralyzed. You left. I tried to look for you, but Twenty brought me here."

"Oh, believe me, I was only trying to get you help, Rain. I'm so sorry."

"It's not your fault."

"Are you okay?"

"Not really."

She was shaking so bad, and the fear in her eyes was so vivid, I had to say something to try and calm her down "Raina, I really do love you."

"Really? I was worried last night...well, I don't know."

Suddenly my feelings were very clear. Raina wasn't some girl I had just kissed on a whim. I had never believed in love at first sight. How could love just suddenly blossom in such a fashion? It did though. One moment it was a seed resting in a jar waiting to be planted. The next thing it was a grove of flowers reaching for the sun, their scent as intoxicating as wine. "Last night was the best night of my life; I never expected us to be friends. I actually expected us to hate each other among all this pain and suffering, but you're far too lovely to hate."

"I knew I loved you the moment I saw you. I just wanted you so badly. You're like this drug you get addicted to just by looking at that. But then that isn't enough. You want more and more; you want to experience that drug." She looked flustered and upset as if she had said something wrong.

To ease the tension, I leaned down and kissed her. Yes, I most certainly loved her. Twenty chose that moment to show up. "Well, it's nice to see you, Nicole. Did you and my wolf have fun last night?"

I raised my knife up trying to keep my grip on it. My hand was shaking badly. "Leave us alone."

"I see you brought my knife back. Thank you, my dear." He held out his hand.

"I'll stab you."

"Go ahead." His gaze hardened. I dropped the knife into his outstretched palm feeling weak and stupid. I wasn't going to defeat Twenty anytime soon. "Now you can stand over there."

"Why? What are you going to do?"

He pushed past me and went to Raina gently pulling up her shirt. "Xephius used to do this with a scythe. This will be less painful."

"What are you doing?" I tried to move, but I found myself paralyzed.

"Don't worry, Raina. Things will be all right," he whispered his voice soft and almost kind.

She started to scream, and at first, I didn't understand why. Then I saw a long spear like needle sticking deep into her stomach. "It hurts," she hissed. "It's going to kill me." I had never heard her voice like that; it was screechy like sandpaper. He ripped the needle out, and the blood sprayed over himself and her. Her body went limp, and her eyes closed.

Feeling myself free as the constricting feeling vanished I ran to her side. Running my hands over her face, murmuring her name repeatedly. She was out cold. "Why did you do that? You're going to kill her baby."

"No, her baby is going to die if I do not do that. As female humans go for ultrasounds that is what Raina must do."

"Is she okay?"

"I'm afraid she is having severe complications."

"Can I do anything?"

"Yes, you can show her love and take care of her."

He carried her back to my room and laid her underneath the covers. "She needs you now. Magic isn't going to help her."

I wanted to ask him so much and beg him to at least try and fix her, but he vanished before I had the chance.

"What's going on?" Raina struggled to sit up and push the covers off.

"It's okay. You're going to be fine."

"I'm so hot."

I put the back of my hand against her forehead and then jumped back waving my hand as the burning pain scorched my palm. I'd say she was hot! Her skin was unbearable to touch. "Don't worry, Rain. I'll take care of you."

Four Months Later

As Raina's pregnancy wore on, I lost all sense of time. The only thing I was really aware of was that I was truly losing her. With each passing day, she grew weaker and weaker until she could scarcely bring herself to get out of bed. Her stomach grew, and her skin stretched to hold the baby. Unfortunately, her symptoms were also growing: pain tore through her so excruciating she would scream for hours on end. Walking was nearly impossible, and she couldn't keep a thing down. She went from happily eating everything in sight to barely choking down dry toast.

I did everything I could to take care of her, from helping her wash her tearstained face and telling her stories so she could drift into sleep. My stories always made her smile and seemed to calm her. I, on the other hand, slept very little and found no way to calm myself. Would she and her helpless infant ever be okay?

Then one morning she just sat up in her bed smiling as if nothing had been wrong. "So, how's Hershey been?"

For a moment, I was dumbfounded. "He's fine."

"And you and Marley?"

"Everything's okay, but how are you?"

"Starving."

That made sense. She hadn't eaten much these past few months. "You think your stomach can handle some food?"

"Oh, yes, I'd like one of those mushroom steaks you were always talking about. Oh, and where are our little rascals? Can you bring them in here?"

"No problem. I'll go ask Twenty."

Truth be told I wasn't looking forward to asking anything of Twenty. He had taken care of Hershey and Marley while I had cared for Raina. He had been kind enough to leave us alone—no torture or anything.

After walking around aimlessly for a few minutes, I found him in one his favourite places, the room he called his study. The room was pleasant: books mounted on the walls, a grand desk with heavy wooden chairs, and walls that were deep red.

"Well, Nicole, how are you?"

"All right. A little tired."

"I am certain you are more than a little tired. Don't worry. You will have time to rest. Raina must be feeling better since she would like food. I have her meal prepared. And also your little animals have had some fun these past few months." With a snap of his fingers, they came running out from behind the desk and came barreling toward me. I dropped down to my knees allowing them to lick my face and climb on my lap. "Okay, guys, go see Raina."

Marley jumped over Hershey, and then they were both off crashing down the hall.

Twenty and I had shared a light laugh before he handed me a plate holding the extra-large portabella mushroom. It was so big that I would have thought it was actually meat. On the side was a heaping pile of mashed potatoes drowned in golden butter.

"Thank you."

He wasn't through though. He handed me a wrapped package that I accepted gingerly as if it may have been an active bomb.

"What's this?"

"Raina is nine months pregnant. She will be having her baby soon. This book will help you prepare."

"All right."

"You will do fine."

"Why can't you help her? She's having a baby, for crying out loud. How am I supposed to help her?"

"Read the book. For countless years women have been midwives for other women. Now go take Raina her meal."

When I got back to the room, Hershey and Marley were curled up comfortably among the quilts, and Raina was sitting upwards, her bulging belly exposed.

"Here you go," I said passing her the plate of food. She had eaten everything in ten minutes flat; she truly must have been starving. That plate was so clean one could never have guessed that it had been used. She wiped her face and sat there smiling contentedly.

"Twenty gave me this book that will help us deliver your baby."

She looked down. "What if I can't do it? What if she dies?"

"Don't worry. We'll figure everything out."

For over an hour we pored over the very thick book. Apparently, Bloodens didn't give birth in the normal sense. No, of course not. Their babies broke through their stomachs with thirty knives. This was going to be fun. The rest of the book described how to endure the lengthy labour.

"Can we do this?" she asked.

I let out a shaky breath. "I sure hope so because this is going to happen whether we're ready or not. We have this book. It's going to be okay."

"Of course." She leaned over and stroked Hershey, who was curled up beside Marley. They looked peaceful. Of course, after their nap, they turned into raging whirlwinds. For the rest of the day, we lounged around and entertained the energetic duo cheering them on as they ran laps around the room, making Raina laugh happily. I watched as the worry vanished and a beautiful energy filled her body. Her joyful mood made me feel equal to her.

Times like this made me forget the cruel misery of the world; suddenly my thoughts were interrupted by Marley jumping up onto my lap and knocking me over in my vulnerable state. Hershey was in the position of trying to eat my hair.

Raina just sat there laughing at me. When I finally managed to get the psychotic nuts off me, she was sitting there still laughing.

"Just because you're pregnant doesn't mean you can sit there and act like a dead fish."

"A dead fish," she giggled.

"Yes, a dead fish."

"Calm your pickles, moo moo."

"Are you calling me a cow?"

"Yes, moo."

"At least I'm not a hippo," she grinned jokingly.

"Oh, but hippos rule. They smell like pineapples."

"No, they do not."

"In my mind they do."

We laughed so hard that we both doubled over. This conversation was so ridiculous. We were getting tired, so we pulled up the blankets and snuggled together, our furry animals between us. Before I knew it I drifted into a deep, peaceful sleep. Hours later though I awoke to horrific screams.

Raina had thrust the blankets off and was lying on her back, the cries of pain fleeing from her mouth as ten sparkling knives had broken through her stomach.

"Oh God."

"Help me. It hurts so badly."

"You're in labour."

"Yes, you idiot. What do you think is happening?"

The knives had come through about one inch. Twenty-nine more inches to go. How was I going to help her? I decided to start with something simple; her hair was hanging onto her face, so I took an elastic band and tied it back. Pulling a tissue off of the nightstand I wiped away her tears.

"I'm scared," she whispered.

"It's going to be fine. You can do this."

She screamed as pain tore through her. "We live with a monster. How can I bring my little girl into this?"

"This isn't your fault. You didn't get pregnant on purpose." Her screams drowned out what I was trying to say.

That's when Twenty showed up. "You have to help us," I cried trying to keep the hysteria in my voice to a minimum. Now wasn't a time to panic.

"Here is a knife to cut the umbilical cord and clean blankets for the baby."

"Don't leave."

"Goodbye."

"Wait." But he was already gone.

I took a deep breath and looked to Raina. She wasn't screaming anymore, but her head was bac, and her eyes were closed. The knives were out about ten inches now. I held her hand tightly as if I could leech the pain into my own body; she lay there like that for hours as the knives tore through her bit by bit. She cried at first but eventually gave into the pain. Finally, though the knives reached a full thirty inches, I felt like a naïve child as the thought crossed my mind, how was the baby getting out? I tried to remember what the book said, but all I could think of was how sadistic knives had such a metallic gleam.

"How the heck is this baby getting out?"

Raina was so weak the words barely managed to pass her lips. "The knives... they'll move."

Oh, and that they did. In mere seconds, they sunk within the wounds they had risen from and twisted violently to the side as they rose. Raina screamed along the new wave of pain, pressing her hands against her ribs as if to make it all go away. I reached to take her hand just as one of the knives had swayed to the side slashing my throat open.

The strangled cry escaped my mouth as I stepped back waiting for the knives to move once again, but that's when I realized the knives were gone and a hole had opened up within her stomach. I reached my hands into this hole and pulled out ever so carefully the little baby. She was so small, her hands curled up as if she were praying. I severed the umbilical cord and wiped the blood from her body. As I cleaned her, I knew something was horribly wrong. She wasn't crying; that meant she wasn't breathing.

Blood from my face dripped down onto her face. I went to wipe it away, but then I realized her eyes were open and she was blinking. I started to rock her, to bounce her up and down, to do anything to get her stimulated. She made a little coughing noise and then spit up blood all over me. Finally, she was crying. I grabbed one of the clean blankets and wrapped her up.

Raina's stomach had healed, and she was struggling to sit up. "Oh my God."

Gently I passed Raina her little bundle of joy. The little Blooden was beautiful; she had a perfect round face and a full soft head of black hair. As Raina held her, the little girl's olive, green eyes opened, and she smiled. She held a remarkable resemblance to her mother.

"Do you know what you want to call her?"

"Mary, yes, her name is Mary."

"Like Bloody Mary," I joked.

She smiled thoughtfully. "I don't really have a last name, but I would like her middle name to be Nicole."

"Really!"

"Do you like the name?"

"Of course, I do."

Suddenly, Hershey and Marley, who had stayed out of the way the whole time, decided that they needed to come and see. They were all over little Mary licking her face and nuzzling against her. She ran her fingers over their fur and smiled. She was so perfect: truly and absolutely perfect.

The next morning Raina and I both slept late. The bed was free of blood, and our room had changed: there was a crib for Mary along with a small wardrobe full of clothes for her. Raina and I ended up in plain white dresses while we dressed Mary in a small purple dress fringed with white lace.

After Raina had fed her, we sat down on the bed laying her between us. She was remarkable.

"I can't believe you did it. You really did."

"Well, you helped. You took such good care of me. How can I ever repay you?"

"Oh, I can think of a few ways," I said smiling as our lips met.

The night Raina was exhausted after caring for Mary. She collapsed onto the bed. As I watched her, it was almost impossible to stop from smiling. I sat beside her and caressed her cheek, tracing the outline of her face. Her eyes opened for a second, but I told her to go back to sleep. After all, she had just brought a little person into the world; she deserved her rest.

Speaking of that little person, she needed me. I pulled her carefully from her crib and held her gently to calm her cries. Even as I rocked her in my arms, she still whimpered, so I began to sing her a lullaby that my mother had often sang to me:

"Go to sleep and dream of me
Sugar plums and apple trees
Baby birds up on their nests
Your kind smile is the best

Even though your day was long
Think of sounds like bingle bong
Breathe and breathe, it's time to sleep
No more talk, no more peeps

A smiling moon and sleeping sun
Your sweet dreams have just begun
See a bakery filled with cakes
And all the things you can make

Go to sleep and dream of me
Sugar plums and apple trees
Baby birds up in their nest

Your kind smile is the best."

When I looked down, she was sound asleep, a smile as beautiful as her mother's splayed across her face. I place her back in her crib and fell into bed beside Raina. Everyone was asleep except for Marley, who was still sort of awake. I decide to talk to him. "I think I would have been a good mother. I love this little baby. Do you think I could eat one of those berries? I mean, I don't know what I'm saying. I'm tired."

He yawned, and with that, we fell asleep.

For about a week we didn't do much. We slept late and entertained Mary. But the strange happiness formed by the innocence of the child was shattered. Twenty showed up, and as usual, the mood changed immediately. There was something especially sadistic about the way he was smiling.

"Well, well, Raina, how are you?"

She looked down self-consciously. "I'm fine."

He placed his hand against her stomach. "The wounds healed nicely. How is your infant?" At the mention of Mary, Raina scooped her up from her spot on the bed and held her close. "Raina, hand me Mary."

"No, please don't hurt her."

"Do you think I am so insensitive that I would harm a baby? Hand her to me."

She looked over at me as if I could possibly help her. "Just give her to him."

Twenty looked different holding her. His face softened, and he looked relaxed. "She is perfectly healthy, and you are well, as you say?"

"I'm fine," she whispered.

"Excellent, then you two have a torture chamber to clean."

"What?" we exclaimed in unison.

"You two are both slaves, so what do you expect?"

I guess I shouldn't have been so shocked. We did belong to him, and we had to do what he asked us. Before I could think about it anymore he whisked us away.

"Clean this." Raina's jaw dropped as she looked around taking in the scene.

The room was beyond filthy. Grime and flesh stuck stubbornly between the cobblestones, and the smell of decay lingered in the air. In the corner were some meagre cleaning supplies. Bleach filled buckets, rags, and toothbrushes. As we cleaned, we talked about Twenty's insanity and trying to find him a mental institution— hopeless thoughts but pleasant talk for passing the time. When the last smear of blood was scrubbed away, we were teleported to another room. We sat on a black leather couch. Two chairs were opposite of us. Seated in one was Twenty. Seated in the other was a woman wearing a velvety black cloak. Her skin was a creamy pale, highlighting her fluorescent amethyst eyes. Beneath her hooded cloak, I could see her hair was styled and pulled back nicely. One pesky strand hung across her forehead. I couldn't figure out why she looked so familiar. That's when it hit me. She looked like Sloane. When I was in Paris, I had met her. She was the beautiful exotic dancer who lived with Noah.

"Care to introduce us?" I asked managing to keep my voice even.

The woman stepped forward confidently and shook both of our hands. "Hello, my name is Livella. You must be Nicole and Raina. It is lovely to meet you. Raina, congratulations! Giving birth is the most remarkable thing a woman can achieve."

"Thank you," Raina said awkwardly.

"Where is the lovely little baby?" Livella asked returning to her seat.

I answered, "She's in our room."

Twenty turned to us. "Go and get her."

As we walked down the corridors into the room we shared, we found Mary sound asleep in her crib; she was so peaceful.

"Nicole, why does Twenty want her? What's with that woman? Why do they want my baby?

I pulled her over to the bed and had her sit down. "Raina, take a deep breath. It will be okay."

"She's my baby." Hysteria had risen in her voice with a hint of defiance.

"Don't worry."

"I don't want them to hurt her."

"Why don't we just wake her up and then we'll go from there? You know, I love her just as much you do."

Tears welled up in those beautiful eyes, and like water breaking through a dam, they flooded down her face. I kissed her gently and ran my hand over her hair. "It's okay, my love." Great. Now I sounded ridiculous as well as faltering. I lifted Mary as if she were made of porcelain and would easily shatter. Her little eyes opened, and she smiled when she saw us. That was too much for Raina, and she started to cry harder.

We weren't allowed to return on our own; we were teleported back to that room, and Mary was sent straight into Livella's arms. I felt myself grasping at the air trying to get her back, but she was gone. I wondered if I would ever hold her again. Before we had a chance to say anything, Twenty spoke. "Livella, the baby, a gift of satisfaction."

"Thank you. Tonight I will form the transformation spell, and we will have another little sorceress in the world." She reached down and gave Mary an affectionate Eskimo kiss. "Who's a sweet girl?"

My heart was racing, and my pulse quickened. "You're giving away Mary? How could you?" The words had been meant to come out in the form of a scream, but instead they were a barely audible whisper. I wanted with every fibre of my being to pull Mary back into my arms, but I was paralyzed as was Raina.

Livella smiled tightly. "Excuse me, everyone. I am going to get us some tea." She passed Mary to Twenty and walked out. Twenty looked intently at Raina and then back to Mary's face fresh with innocence. He stroked her cheeks and ran his cool fingers against her smooth skin, speaking to her quietly.

When Livella appeared, she offered each of us a cup of tea, and when we somehow shook our heads no, Twenty stood up and placed Mary back into her arms. She smiled, this time more relaxed, and hesitated before leaving. At the last moment I thought she would give us back Mary. Instead she turned and kissed Twenty right on the lips. He even kissed her back; she smiled again, and then just like that, she was gone.

As quickly as I was puzzled, I was sent back to utter devastation. She had taken Mary with her; our little Mary was gone. Had I even told her that I loved her? What about Raina? Oh, she knew this was going to happen. She just knew.

She had fallen to the ground. She was convulsing and crying in horror that her baby was gone. At least I had never seen my twins. They were just taken away from me. I had no attachment to them. Unfortunately, we both loved Mary, and to Raina having her taken away must have felt like having her very soul ripped out.

Before I could say or do anything she jumped to her feet and started screaming profanities at Twenty in the midst of her rage. "Oh, just what we need—another sorceress in the world. How could you send my baby away? She was mine! You had no right."

He grabbed her wrist as she was about to strike him. "Calm down," he commanded.

"I hate you. You're a horrible person. For God's sake, why don't you just kill me?"

Out of nowhere, his golden dagger appeared, and he thrust it forcefully against her throat. "Death is most often worse than life itself."

Chapter Twenty

We were in our bedroom, but it felt empty and foreign with all the baby stuff gone.

"Raina, I know this is hard, but it's going to work out." She didn't say anything. She just turned away and curled up on the bed beside Hershey. "Rain," I repeated.

"Please, I just need some time."

"Okay," I sighed, but it was best just to do as she wished. As I walked from the room and tried to figure out where to go I heard soft footsteps following close behind me. He ran up to me, and I immediately dropped down to hug him. "I'm sorry, bud. I know I haven't been paying much attention to you lately. How about we go outside?" Outside was a magic word, and he immediately perked up, but he took off running the wrong way. Usually, we went out the front entrance, which led to the meadow. What the heck, though? Hershey and Marley seemed to be much more confident navigating the lengthy confusing passages of the castle. After following him for a short while, we ended up at a heavy wooden door. "This must be some sort of back exit. This is where you want to go."

He barked and jumped up in excitement. "Okay, okay, hold your horses." As I pushed the door open I was met with something beautiful— real sunlight, warm and bright. The grass beneath my feet was green. Oh, this was perfect: real colours like from my funeral dream. I pinched myself and found the corners of my mouth lifting up in a pleased smile. This wasn't a dream. This was a beautiful reality. In the distance was a pond surrounded by willows that seemed to be reaching to the heavens. There was also a greenhouse filled with what appeared to be black roses.

It was all so beautiful. I realized the scenery had distracted me. What did my little Marley think of all this? He was near the greenhouse running, his shaggy fur being blown by a gentle breeze, but he wasn't alone. I first saw only the black and figured it was a shadow. Of course, it wasn't a shadow; it was the wolf running beside him, the wolf that towered over him and could kill my little Marley so easily.

"No, please." The words came out as a hopelessly confused whisper.

"Nicole, it's all right." Twenty came out of the greenhouse and walked calmly toward me.

"Please, don't hurt Marley."

"I've become quite fond of Marley. I would never hurt him and neither would Candlemas."

"Candlemas?"

"My wolf. He has a name."

"That's what they used to call—"

"Groundhog Day, yes."

I looked back at the scene. Marley dropped his front legs down, and Candlemas did the same. They were playing.

"You took Mary away." The bitter words escaped my mouth before I could stop them.

"Come with me."

I followed him into the greenhouse and found I was right. The flowers were black roses. Through the black of their petals was the redness of blood.

"You're right, my dear. These roses were red. I used root dye to dye them black."

"They're pretty. They suit here well enough."

The roses were arranged in thick beautiful clusters; the fragrance they held was delightful. I was content to stay within the realm of my own thoughts, but Twenty had other intentions of drawing me back to reality. "Livella is someone from my past. Her daughter is grown up, and she wanted another baby. I told her I could help her."

"You used Raina as a surrogate. You're as bad as Kyle."

Something akin to anger crossed his face, but it vanished as quickly as it appeared. "Did I rape Raina?"

"No."

"Did I even have her eat the vevlakaneeshnek berry?"

"No."

"Livella will take care of Mary. She will be okay." He smiled and put his hand on my face. "Now why are you out here instead of with Raina?"

"She wanted to be alone."

"Do you really think that?"

"I don't know. It's just hard."

"You've always tried to bury your feelings, and now that is becoming more and more difficult."

"I don't want to be weak."

"That will never happen. Don't worry."

We walked back outside where Marley and Candlemas had finished running and were now lying in the warmth of the sunlight.

"Things will be okay, Nicole. I promise you," he said and with a flick of his wrist Marley and I found ourselves back in our room.

Raina sat up and tried to smile. "I'm sorry," her voice shook, and a new river of tears flowed down her face. I sat on the bed and wrapped my arms around her. We tried talking, but we were both too sad for that, so we curled up enjoying each other's warmth until we fell asleep.

It must have been the middle of the night because when I woke up, it was much darker than usual. I was lying down on that stupid metal table, secured by those unbreakable cuffs. And of course, I was wearing yet another bikini.

"Twenty, where are you?"

"I'm everywhere."

"What kind of stunt is this?"

He showed up at that moment. "Stunt. I'm glad to know you think so little of me."

"You are horrible; you give away Mary, and now you have to torture me. What about mourning time?"

"I happen to think the pain will make you feel more alive." That's when burning pain scorched through my mouth. Acid spilled past my lips and mingled with my tears, attacking my flesh as I screamed.

"Oh, make it stop."

"Why? We're just starting to have fun. I'll be right back; I enjoy leaving you with your thoughts."

And then he was gone. Whatever thought I had must have occurred in milliseconds because he returned in moments with a gleaming knife that stretched as long as my arm. His flesh knife.

He shoved the knife deep into my shoulder until he hit the bone. My blood was a rich river of scarlet fragmented with pieces of bones. My screams tore through the air shattering the waves of silence. He ripped the knife down taking a large strip of my flesh with it.

Tired of mutilating my arm he moved to my stomach making deep, precise cuts. The blade sunk deep inside of me. As he removed it I saw what I believed to be my organs fall upon the table. My heart was pounding and beating so fast I was certain this would be the time it would stop. The thought was so plain and so simple it comforted me like a warm blanket on a cool night.

I let out a strangled, tight scream hoping it would stop the ever-intensifying pain. He slit open my chest so now I could see my heart working painstakingly to pump blood. The sight was sickening. The comforting thoughts of death vanished.

He set his blade down and ran his fingers through the blood; he whispered words of comfort into my ear. "Just a little more, and you can go to Raina." He reached down into my ribs into the deep wound.

"No," I shrieked. He was holding my heart. My freaking heart was out of my body. I couldn't bear it anymore, and mercifully I lost consciousness.

The next thing I was aware of was I was lying on the bed screaming my head off thinking I was still in pain.

"Nicole, wake up." Raina sat beside me and shook my shoulders until I opened my eyes and looked around trying to sort out what was real. "What's wrong?"

"He ripped out my heart. Is it even there? Did he take it away?" I knew I sounded childish, but I was also ridiculously scared.

She placed her hand against my chest. "I can feel it; your heart is still there."

I closed my eyes and sighed. "Life is so screwed up."

"Maybe we just need to be together."

I opened one eye suspiciously. "What do you mean?"

She got up and went to the wardrobe pulling out two packages wrapped in crinkly paper. "Twenty gave these to me after he discovered our updated relationship status. In a place like this, we need happiness. Maybe we just need to bond closer." She removed the paper and left me staring at well. I wasn't really sure.

"Undergarments."

"It's lingerie, silly."

I had to admit the lingerie was very pretty and surprisingly comfortable. I put on the black bra and underwear fringed with white lace. I had never worn anything like that before. Raina's was red as the sunset with the same white lace.

We curled up together, our arms wrapped around one another. Her lips pressed against mine were smooth, her saliva sweet like strawberries. I ran my hands down her sides. "You know what they say? Less is more." I let my head fall back as she kissed my neck. "When I was with Kyle I thought I would never want anyone to touch me."

"Well, I'm glad you've changed your mind," she said with a smile as her bra came undone.

Chapter Twenty-One

As the days passed into weeks, I found myself falling more and more in love with Raina and more accepting of my strange life. We played with the animals and would talk for hours. I suppose I was also more accustomed to everything because it seemed as if Twenty were fading away. I couldn't even remember the last time one of his knives had met my skin.

One day when our buds were especially restless, we took them on a nice long walk, which was another one of our favourite past-times. The bleak sun felt almost warm on this particular day. We ended up past the market and found ourselves at a church.

Raina looked thoughtful as we ventured inside. "Do you believe in God?"

"I used to, but I could never picture God existing in a place like this."

"I had a rosary once. Its beads were like pearls. I don't know what happened to it." She sighed. "I'm kind of tired. Do you think we should head back?"

"Actually, could you take these two back? I wanted to walk a bit more, you know, by myself."

"Why?"

"Ever since we spent that night together Twenty hasn't tortured us, and we barely see him."

"That's good, right?"

"No, I think he's planning something, and after it happens things are going to change."

"After what happens?"

"Something." I bit down hard on my lip to stop the tears that were forming.

"Can I tell you something?"

"Of course?"

"Twenty has never tortured me. He's shoved needles in my stomach to check the baby, and he tattooed my hand, but that's it. He's never done what he does to you."

"Wait, why?"

"I don't think he's ever tortured anyone else but you."

"But what about all those rooms we clean?"

"Well, you know how powerful his magic is."

"Are you suggesting it's all an illusion?"

"Yes, I am," she said. "Enjoy your walk." Her words had turned cold.

As she turned away, I grabbed her shoulder to make her stop. "Why are you angry?"

"I'm not angry. I'm scared. I think you're right." I couldn't tell if she was telling the truth or not. Her face was a mask of bitter indifference. Not knowing what else to say I just watched her red cloak flutter as she walked away, Hershey and Marley at her heels.

I collapsed to the ground and sobbed into the fabric of my own cloak. We had never fought before, and I wasn't even entirely sure this was a fight. All I knew was I was very confused.

As I walked back to the market, the hustle of the crowd was strangely comforting. This market was one of many in the Shadow Lands, but it was my favourite. It had an almost medieval feel to it. Straw on the worn down grass, shacks selling items, people milling around in unusual dress.

As I walked along, I debated whether I should return to the castle. The crowd thickened, and I followed the same path as everyone else. Maybe I should have thought about what kind of people I was walking among: people that weren't really people at all, with the darkest fantasies lingering in the corners of their minds.

People began to stop and stand in front of this sort of wooden stage. I could still see what was happening. Actually, I heard her cries before I saw her, a young half clothed emaciated woman. Her skin was covered in cuts, and her eyes were racked with fear. I didn't move though. Before I could think a man approached her from behind and tore her throat clear open.

"No," I screamed, and before I could stop myself, I was on the stage kneeling next to the lifeless body. I should have left. I should have never been there in the first place, but my mind was not working in my favour today.

"Well, well, what's this?" The man, or should I say Mecrathin, seized the back of my cloak and pulled me roughly to my feet. He leaned closer to me, and I could see how truly awful he was. His skin was set with deep hard lines, his eyes were bloodshot, his hair greasy and tangled, his breath reeking of gin. "Would you like to join her?"

I tried to turn away, but he grabbed my arm and squeezed my skin so tightly I cried out in pain. "Let go. You're hurting me."

"I'll show you hurt." He pulled out a butcher knife and cut a deep gash in my arm. Tears flooded down my face, and I could feel my pulse quicken. "Let's give the crowd a show."

"Maybe you should look at her hand first." Twenty appeared suddenly at the mere threat of my safety. "What is your name?"

"Charlen."

"Well, Charlen, are you blind?"

"No."

Twenty held up my palm. "Then you see this cross, correct?"

"Yes."

"It means she belongs to me." He released my hand and looked down at his hand, which was smeared with my blood. He frowned, and I wondered why wasn't he used to having blood on his skin? "Nicole, pull down your sleeve for me." As I pushed the fabric of my cloak down I saw how truly deep the cut was. Blood was actually spilling to the ground. He ran his hands over the wound healing it immediately. "That wasn't blood, was it? Surely she must have gotten red paint on herself. I know she would never cut herself, and that wound looked very deliberate."

"Yes."

"Now tell me. Did you cut her?" I could hear his voice rising and his eyes flashing greener than ever with anger.

"Yes."

Just like that, he had his golden dagger, and it was shoved deep into Charlen's rib case. "Now you see this knife isn't overly sharp as it is made of gold, but the tip is very sharp, and it is pressed right against your heart. You and I are about to come to an agreement. You will walk away, and I will never see you here again. And if I do see you here I will cut out your still beating heart, shove it down your throat and watch as you swallow your life. Are we understood?"

"Yes, yes." The golden dagger vanished leaving Charlen without injury as he ran in fear. As we stepped off the stage we were met with applause. I guess we had put on a better show. When we were almost back at the castle, I turned and wrapped my arms around him. "Thank you. You're really becoming my saviour."

He looked surprised. "You're welcome."

"I am sorry. I know you have warned us about going to the market alone. Why did he kill that girl?"

"That is called a slicing, a public killing."

"I apologize. Please don't be mad." Seeing Twenty so livid in such a controlled fashion was alarming.

"I'm not mad. Besides, he wouldn't have been able to kill you."

"Would you be able to kill me?" As the question left my mouth I wasn't even sure why I had asked. I didn't want to die. Instead of answering he held out a small black box.

"What's this?"

"Well, why don't you open it and find out?"

I smiled to myself and carefully pulled it open. "Oh my gosh." It was a beautiful ring with two pearls held beside each other. One black as the cloak I was wearing, the second white and shimmering. A closer look revealed they were held by two silver hands. Yes, hands so detailed with smooth wrists pressed against each other and fingers resting over the pearls in their palms. "This is exquisite. Where did you get this?"

"Well, you know that quaint little flower shop on Avenue Five a few blocks from there?" He was being sarcastic.

"Would you shut up?"

"Perhaps."

I looked intently at the ring knowing it would never fit on one of my fingers; the band was far too small. I could see Raina wearing it though. She would have a true appreciation for the magnificent pearls. "You want me to give this to Raina."

"Do *you* want to give this to Raina?"

"We had a fight today."

"What about?"

"Why don't you just read my mind?"

"Well, I could do that about every single thing you think about, and we would never have any more conversations."

"Fine, it was about you."

"Interesting." He smiled so strangely, in a fashion that suggested narcissism, that I burst out laughing.

"We both agree you must be plotting something but what?"

"Well, I'm not sure what am I plotting."

"Great, you don't even know. You've hardly been around lately. What are you doing? Maybe you go into the human world and walk through walls to scare people."

This time he laughed. "I'm just away, that's all." As we stood at the entrance of the castle he stopped me and put his hand around my throat. I thought he was going to choke me but he didn't.

"What are you doing?"

"I can feel your blood moving."

"Okay then."

I think we stood there for a few more minutes, and I had to admit I felt strangely comforted; when he pulled his hand away I found myself thinking *don't stop.* "Now go to Raina."

"Wait. Where are you going?"

"Oh, I don't know. I might walk through some walls and scare people." With that he disappeared leaving me with my thoughts.

As I walked through the corridors and back to our room, I wondered what to do. Maybe she wasn't really mad at me, and I was overreacting, but on the other hand, there was a certain chilliness in her voice that I had never heard before.

"Raina," I said softly standing hesitantly at the doorway. "Rain, are you mad? Do you want to talk?"

She was lying on the bed, her back toward me. I walked over to her only to find she wasn't ignoring me; she was asleep curled up beside Hershey. My heart nearly skipped a beat with relief over the fact that she wasn't blocking me out.

A steady thump, thump behind me caught my attention. My little Marley. I knelt down and wrapped my arms around him, clinging to him as if my life depended on it. "I don't know what to do. I can never fix anything. I want Dad back." As the words left my mouth, I was hit by way of memories: him taking me to get my special haircut on my birthday, teaching me how to do a pull-up and just taking care of me. He was always there. I couldn't have asked for a better father. Why didn't I tell him I loved him more often? Why did I think he would always be there when now I would never see him again?

I don't know where the sudden pain came from, but it hit hard and attacked with a vicious vengeance. I wanted him back so bad I couldn't take it. Tears flooded down my face in bucketfuls, and pent up screams escaped from within.

"Nicole." The only person that may have mattered found me and wrapped her arms around my trembling body. "What's wrong?"

"I want him back. It's not fair."

"Your dad, right?"

"I didn't do anything right. I took him for granted."

She took my hand and guided me to the bed "I don't believe that. You're so kind. I know you love me, and I'm certain he knew how much you loved him." Hershey and Marley jumped up beside us. "I know the pain is horrific, and it never truly leaves, but just think of a good memory and tell me."

"All right." I stopped for a second to wipe my eyes and compose myself. "Um, I used to get really sick a lot, high fevers, awful nausea. He would stay up with me all night and tell me about his work training soldiers, his tours of Afghanistan. I wanted to go into the military, so I loved these stories. Plus he made the best dinners. He was a wonderful cook. He did a great job of fulfilling the role of both parents. For a guy he loved flowers: narcissus, lilac, roses, and lilies were his favourite."

"Do you feel better?"

"Yes, what would I do without you?" We kissed, and as I pulled away I felt an intense pressure in my right hand. A quick glance revealed the ring resting between my fingers. I held it up in front of her "Do you like it?"

"Oh my gosh, it's beautiful."

"Well, would you like to have it?"

"Yes." She reached to take it, but I pulled it back.

"You have to answer a trivia question to get it."

"Okay then."

"Will you marry me?"

She shrieked so loud that my ears rung. Without warning she pushed me backward kissing my face over and over.

"Calm down before you give yourself a heart attack." I pushed myself into a sitting position and slid the ring onto her left ring finger. "You and I will be together for now and all eternity."

"I wonder what that will be like when we're a thousand."

"Or a million." At that we both burst into laughter.

A week later I stood in an exceptionally lavished room, wearing only a thin white robe. I was waiting to see what my wedding dress would look like. After I had proposed to Raina and Twenty came to congratulate us, I told him the wedding should happen soon, very soon. I hated when people got engaged and then waited months to marry. I think if we had waited any more than a week I would have exploded with excitement.

Raina and I had decided we wouldn't see each other until the ceremony so our first night being married would be even more special. I kept my sanity by helping Twenty plan everything. The cake was in the shape of a curled up snake: a yellow Burmese python to be exact.

We had two flower girls—the sweetest little Mecrathins, Zoë and Willow. I met them once, and the pleasure of seeing children was similar to lighting a lantern in a field of unbearable darkness. They were about six with long blonde hair, pink flushed cheeks, and beautiful kind eyes; they were the picture of innocence, young souls untouched by the capricious nature of life.

Raina had worked out other details. She had asked Twenty if it was okay to use my Dad's favourite flowers: narcissus, lilac, roses, and lilies. He and I both agreed that would work perfectly. She had also worked with Hershey while I worked with Marley teaching them to walk down the aisle. Yes, everything was going to be exceptional. But where was Twenty? I was tired of standing around in this skimpy robe. Just as I plopped down into a cushioned red chair he appeared.

"Where were you? I've been waiting."

"I don't know. Walking through walls and scaring people."

"Ha ha. Rather funny. Where is my dress? You didn't even let me pick it out."

He took my hands and pulled me to my feet. "You will love it. Now close your eyes."

Just as my eyelids shut the robe vanished, and I could feel the dress resting against my skin. With my eyes still closed, Twenty took my hand and led me to the other side of the room. "Okay, now look."

I had worn many dresses before, but none were as beautiful as this. No, the person staring back at me couldn't have been me. This dress had no sleeves or straps; the fabric simply wrapped itself perfectly around my chest. The bodice was covered, both front and back, with shimmering pearls that complemented the creamy white of the fabric beneath them. The bottom flowed out princess style but fell just above my feet so I wouldn't trip. "I love it."

"Don't forget your shoes, Cinderella."

I seized the shoes he was holding out eagerly. "Glass. Oh, I've always wanted a pair of glass slippers." I put them on and they fit perfectly.

"I know."

"Okay, how do you know all this? Were you stalking me my entire life?"

"No, I found you when you were about thirteen exploring the mountain paths, reading your books. You were perfect."

"But you didn't take me then."

"No, I wanted you to experience your childhood and take you as you bordered the fine line of becoming an adult."

"Okay then, so what's Raina's dress look like?"

"I can't tell you that. You know the groom isn't supposed to see the bride."

"Thanks a lot." What he said actually stung. I looked down at my feet.

He pushed my chin up gently. "Only teasing, my dear. You are far too beautiful to be a man. Now come, you and Raina will be walking down the aisle soon."

"I'm nervous."

"Don't be." He put his hand around my throat just for a second, and then we were standing in a small dimly lit room. "Now you and Raina will walk in through those doors over there, and I will guide you through the entire ceremony. Everything will be perfect."

As he vanished Raina appeared. Now she was an exquisite creature. Beautiful could not come close to accurately describing her. Her dress was a brilliant ivory; a soft white panel with crisscross purple ribbons went down her chest. The neckline was a V but didn't go down too low, and the sleeves ran just past her elbow and lightly frilled out with purple fabric that matched the purple crisscross. Where my dress's bottom was light, hers was full and covered her feet completely.

"Oh my gosh, you're beautiful," we said in unison.

I smiled. "I thought it was nice that you picked out my dad's favourite flowers. Really, that means a lot."

"Well, you worked really hard to plan things. Nice job with the cake. Twenty said it's a snake."

"Yes, a Burmese python, a yellow one all curled up."

"I hate snakes. They're creepy."

"Well, it's marble cake, with vanilla custard, and buttercream frosting."

"That's better."

I wrapped my arms around her and pulled her close. "I'm so happy now."

"I never thought I would see this day, not with where I used to be. Xephius was so mean to me."

I stepped back and saw the tears that threatened to spill over her long eyelashes "He's dead, Raina, and he will never be able to hurt you again unless you deny yourself happiness."

"You're right. This is the best day of my life."

I ran my hand over the back of her head, and that's when I realized how fancy her hair was done. The longest strands twisted into braids. The rest curled down her back flowing like a magnificent waterfall.

"Your hair is so beautiful."

"Twenty did it for me."

"Could you turn around?" As she did I found myself looking at how someone who could turn my skin into a blood stained array of cuts could use his patience and creativity to create such beauty. "Wow."

"I know," she said turning to face me. "He's got some neat tricks, huh?"

"I'm just glad he's given me you."

At that, our lips met, and I knew that no one, man or woman, could possibly replace her. Our moment together was soon interrupted by a shrill shriek. Zoë and Willow stood behind us giggling hysterically.

"You two are so beautiful," Zoë gushed.

"I can't wait for the wedding to begin," Willow added shyly.

I knelt down beside them. "You two are also beautiful." They were wearing lovely little dresses with cute puffy sleeves.

As I stood back up Zoë began to talk a mile a minute. "I was so excited for this day. We invited our entire class from school to come. Even the boys. Boys are so yucky."

"Well, not all of them."

"I thought you would agree with me since you are marrying a girl."

Raina immediately noticed how uncomfortable I was and quickly changed the topic. "Do you guys have your flowers?"

"Oh, yes," they said together.

The bouquets were spectacular—lilacs with their many flowers all clustered together, black roses with hints of blood red, narcissus with white petals and centres that looked like shooting stars waiting to jet across the sky, and the ever so delicate purple lilies that looked so outer worldly.

And then Hershey and Marley showed up with their bow tie collars sending the little girls into a spiral of excitement all over again. I was beginning to grow anxious. Why was everything taking so long? Just as I was about to ask Raina, loud bells began to toll.

"That's our cue," she said.

"Wait. Why didn't Twenty tell me the cue?"

The doors opened on their own, and Hershey and Marley with their training drilled into them. They started to walk, then Zoë and Willow, then us.

I looped my arm through Raina's, and as we entered the room, we were both awestruck. Twenty had set everything up perfectly; there was a little church area where everyone was sitting, a floor for dancing, and a table covered with our cake and other sorts of food, surrounded by small tables for people to sit.

I think we were both a little stunned and forgot what we were supposed to do, but I guess we must have remembered because the next thing I knew we were walking forward. All I kept thinking was I couldn't believe this was happening. By the time we reached Twenty, Zoë and Willow were seated in two ornately detailed chairs, our little buds sitting promptly at their feet.

We stood at a small table. A wooden bowl and gleaming silver dagger rested upon it. Twenty was direct and started immediately. "We are here today to witness the joining of two souls together for now and all eternity."

His voice was clear and gentle as he directed us. We stuck our wrists into the water purifying and numbing the skin we were to slice open. As the wounds bled, we smeared the blood onto each other's lips and recited a long series of vows that neither of us understood. This was followed by the placing of the rings. He made Raina's appear first, and as I slid it onto her finger, her smile melted away any possible bit of unhappiness that may have remained locked within my heart. My ring was simply a gold band, so simple it suited me perfectly.

At last, it was time for us to kiss: the kiss that would join our souls as one. As our lips met, and the taste of her strawberry lip gloss mingled with blood filled my mouth. A horrific pain even worse than contractions tore through my stomach. Raina must have experienced the pain because she fell beside me.

Just as I thought this was just an elaborate plan for Twenty to kill us, the pain vanished all at once leaving only a pleasant sensation behind. He helped us to our feet and healed the wounds on our wrists before turning us to face the crowd.

"Behold two separate souls are now one. Now we celebrate."

Chapter Twenty-Two

Everyone got up, and the crowd seemed to splinter in different directions. Before I had time to thank Twenty again Zoë and Willow ran up to us. "That was excellent. It was so beautiful. You two are the most gorgeous wonderful couple in all of the Shadow Lands," Zoë gushed.

"Thank you," I said smiling. These two were adorable.

"May we play with your animals?" Willow asked shyly.

"Of course," Raina said. "They love attention."

Willow eagerly scooped up Hershey leaving Zoë with Marley, who was not as willing to leave my side to be with someone he didn't know. She gestured for him to come, and when that failed she twisted her fingers and made a small blue ball appear, which immediately made him follow her.

I wrapped my arm around Raina's and watched as Zoë and Willow showed Hershey and Marley to a group of friends. "Children are so rejuvenating, so full of life and innocence."

"I know," she sighed. "I wished we still had Mary."

Before I could think of a response, Twenty appeared. "I have someone I want you to meet." He led us to a small table where the last person I expected to see was seated—Sloane.

We sat down beside her; Raina smiled happily, and I wasn't really sure what to say. Raina, on the other hand, seemed very certain of herself.

"Nicole, Raina, the ceremony was so lovely. Raina, it is good to see you. It's been years. And Nicole, you look so much better since the last time I saw you."

"Wait. I thought you were just a human. You two know each other?"

Raina laughed. "Well, one of my masters would have me sell things in the market. That is where I met Sloane. She was such a good friend. I never thought I would see you again."

"Wait, wait," I said raising my voice slightly. "You're really not a human."

Sloane took a deep breath. "No, I am a sorceress. I just spend much of my time in the human world."

"Are you still living with Noah?"

"Yes, I am."

"How is he?" Noah had been so kind and nice to me.

"He has been better. When he found out about Kyle's death it devastated him. They had been friends since they were very young. Believe me, he wanted to help you, but he was torn between you and his friendship. When he found out Kyle was dead, he was worried about you, and he did phone the police, but he had no idea where you were. He assisted the police though in all ways that he could. The investigation came to a dead-end, and Twenty's spell has slowly erased you away. Magic like that is tricky though, and Noah still sometimes wakes up in the middle of the night trying to sort out a dream about a beautiful young woman who captured his heart."

"I don't know what to say. Is he okay? I mean—"

"I'm sorry. I didn't mean to make you feel uncomfortable. I just didn't want you to hate him or think he was indifferent to your suffering. "

"No, no. I never thought that. I only wish him well."

"In that case, he has found a new love interest."

"Who?"

"Me. We are also expecting."

"Oh my God," Raina and I exclaimed together.

I was still feeling slightly confused about Sloane. "So, not trying to be rude, but what are you doing here?"

"I'm actually visiting my mother. There she is now."

I guess that we both saw her at the same time—Livella. But Livella wasn't by herself. She was carrying a baby, with a thick head of unmistakable black hair, Mary.

Raina began to cry and laugh at the same time eagerly reaching for her daughter. As she cradled her in her arms, I could see our sweet Mary was well looked after. She had grown bigger, and her eyes sparkled with happiness. She was even well dressed wearing a white knitted sweater with pink flowers on the collar, soft pink pants, and those little baby shoes that also had flowers on them that matched her sweater.

We sat across from Livella, the person we previously thought was the devil, but now this. We didn't know what to think now.

"Are you giving her back?" I asked trying to keep the still burning hatred in my voice to a minimum.

"No, but I am here to tell you that you will both be in her life. You'll be able to see her every week. She's growing so fast, already two months old and trying to use magic. She's very easy to mind—slept straight through the night the first day we brought her home. Sloane loves caring for her."

"You'll really let us be a part of her life?" Raina asked barely daring to believe it.

"Of course. You are her mother."

"Oh, thank you. Thank you."

"Well, we do have to be going now. It's time for Mary's nap. You two enjoy yourselves."

Raina gave Mary one last long look before handing her back. "Goodbye, sweetie."

Sloane waved. "Maybe we can all meet up tomorrow and have tea."

Livella smiled. "Yes, I agree. That would work perfectly." With that they were gone.

"Well, that was something," I said trying to sort my feelings into words, but honestly, I think I was too stunned to feel anything.

"Oh, Nicole, it's more than we could have ever hoped for! We have her back." Raina's smile looked as if it were going to jump right off her face.

"We can be parents." As the words left my mouth I knew I wanted to watch Mary grow up and teach her things, but with the slight feeling of happiness and distant hope came a dark sadness and bitter envy. As much as I loved Mary and wanted to be a part of her life, she wasn't mine. I suddenly wanted my twins, *my* little girls. I glanced up and caught Twenty watching me; he gestured for me to come. "Hey, Rain, I'll be right back."

As I approached Twenty the anger that had been building inside me broke through the cage I had tried to lock it in. Unable to control myself I reached to punch him, but as if he were anticipating this, he grabbed my wrist and held tightly until the muscles in my arm relaxed. I stepped back practically shaking with agitation.

"You do know, my dear, that punching isn't very ladylike. You should try a nice open-handed slap."

"I can't do this."

"Can't do what?"

"This," I practically screeched waving my hands around.

"What is wrong?"

"Well, for one, I am very much embarrassing myself. Everybody probably thinks I'm some sort of psychotic lunatic."

"Don't worry. No one saw that. Anything else?"

"I didn't even get to see them. They were just taken away from me, and now they're growing up in that cult."

"Your children?"

I nodded and burst into tears. If I hadn't grabbed onto his arm I would have collapsed. He reached out and put his hand around my throat and then gently wiped away my fallen tears. "It's too happy of a day for you to cry. Come and have some of your wedding cake."

As I followed him to the table of food, I found there was something in his tone that made me feel better as if the sadness were fading away, and there was something beautiful waiting to fill the void.

He handed me a decoratively fancy china plate with a heaping piece of cake, and when we found an empty table, he pulled out my chair for me like a perfect gentleman. "Thank you."

"How's the cake?"

"Oh," I took a large forkful and immediately found myself smiling. The icing was rich and creamy; the light, fluffy cake complemented it perfectly. "This is pure perfection."

"I guess I did a good job then."

"You made this?"

"Why, of course."

"Did you use magic?"

"Yes." His gaze was challenging as if he were daring me to continue.

"Then it doesn't count, but it is delicious."

"Well, to change the subject, I know that you have been worried about your children, but what if I could tell you that they are no longer members of the cult they were born into?"

"What!?"I almost choked.

"After Kyle was killed, Zelda was the one who found his body. She didn't stick around to ask questions. She stole one of the cult's vehicles and left with Kayla and Dren, your little girls. They now have a small house, a stable life, and Zelda has married a kind man who treats her well. They are all very happy."

He slid me a small picture of the two girls; they were probably about a year old sitting around a small table having a tea party with their teddy bears. What really struck me was the fact that they looked just like me. The same light skin tone, hazel eyes, blonde hair although theirs was longer, but even the smile was like mine.

"Oh my God," was all I could manage to say.

"And that's not the only good news. As she was leaving she came across two very distraught young women and offered to give them a ride. I believe their names may have started with an S. If only I could remember what they were."

"Sarah and Starr: they got out?"

"Yes, and Starr had a beautiful baby boy."

"So I really did help them."

"You've done more than you ever could have imagined." His gaze softened. "Now, my dear, go dance with your bride. The music is just beginning."

He was right. As I searched for Raina a sweltering array of notes arose from unseen instruments and lifted everyone's spirits. I found her standing among a group of Shadow Figures. Silently I took her hand and led her through the parted crowds to the centre of the dance floor. We stood staring at each other for a few moments, but as the couples began to find each other and the music played on now with light piano melodies, we came together.

Our feet moved lightly, and we truly seemed to be united as one. I felt somewhat awkward. Dancing had never been one of my skills, so I settled to lead her in small steps that I hoped looked like a waltz. But Raina, always being more confident, twirled around like a ballerina, extending her arms, testing each step, and then just kicking her heels away so she could truly dance.

My mother had loved ballet very much, and we used to watch the different ballets together. Raina looked as if she could be in Swan Lake, which was my absolute favourite. As she approached me out of impulse, I lifted her up by the waist and spun her around. She was as light as a feather. When she found her footing, her face was flushed, and her beautiful smile lit up her eyes like a glowing candle.

As we kissed, I had that feeling of lying on a cliff and being drowned in caramel. Kissing her was exhilarating and sweet. Feeling the adrenaline leave our bodies we held each other close and took small steps that this time felt like waltzing. "You're so beautiful. Where did you ever learn to dance like that?"

"I used to dance all the time, but I have to admit it is much nicer to have a partner."

"Do you want to know something?"

"What?"

"My children, they're safe. Life is really getting better, and that leaves me wondering what married life will be like."

"Pure wonder." She smiled mischievously. "Lots of long nights together, deep conversations, and I hope many kisses."

"I agree."

We continued dancing for maybe half an hour simply allowing ourselves to enjoy the wonders of the beautiful music until Twenty came for us. It was time for drinks and socializing. He led us to another part of the room near the table of food where another man stood. "Nicole, Raina, this is my friend Kemlek."

"Hi," I said softly.

"Hello," Raina added in a short whisper.

I think we were both feeling a little nervous. Twenty had never mentioned any "Kemlek" before, and we had no idea what kind of person he might have been.

"Hello, ladies. It is lovely to meet you." His voice was kind and quiet, practically the opposite of Twenty's tone.

"You look different," I said stumbling. "Not so dreary."

He wore a black dress shirt and grey pants, but his shirt sleeves went down to about his elbows. His complexion was fair, not pale, and his red hair was sort of long and messy. He also didn't seem to be so against colour; he wore a crisp golden tie that enhanced his amber eyes.

"Thank you, Nicole. Most people don't appreciate my fashion sense. Take Twenty, for example. Nothing but black."

"Are you a Mecrathin like Twenty?"

"Well, either one is a Mecrathin like Twenty or they're not, but that's not exactly what I am."

"You don't really look like anyone here. You're like some kind of foreigner."

"You know, Twenty told me about you. I thought it was impossible, but then again you were once a human, so you know something better than this land. You are bound to be unique."

This was suddenly starting to make sense—the way he was dressed, how he spoke: "You're a human?"

"Yes, once upon a time I was."

"How did you end up here?"

"Well, we all have stories."

"What is yours?"

"Hardly anything worth telling." He smiled modestly.

"Tell us," Raina and I said. Our interest was steadily growing. Who was Kemlek?

"I barely know where to begin." He laughed shortly. "I haven't spoken about this in many years. I suppose I should start with the most important element of the story and that would be Peter. The only man I truly loved."

"You're gay," Raina gasped.

"Raina," I hissed. I had hidden my reaction better, but I was also stunned.

"That's quite all right. Learning something like that can be shocking. Neither of our parents took the news very well, and we lost a few good friends. We didn't care though. Our love mattered more than anything to the both of us. Eventually, we got married and had our own house. Life was as perfect as perfect could be. But then everything changed. It was October tenth, and we had just gone out for Chinese food to celebrate our anniversary. As we were walking down Colorado Boulevard, we heard gun shots. The next thing I knew Peter fell to the ground; he'd been shot in the neck. There was chaos, people crying and screaming. I felt so alone, though I knelt beside him and tried to tell him it would be okay. But he knew he was dying. We could hear sirens wailing in the distance; I told him to hang on, and he said he would miss me. I remember looking into his eyes. He was so scared. I kissed him one last time, and I could feel it as the life left his body. The next thing I knew I was sitting in a police station being questioned. I really wasn't much help. I hadn't seen anything. Someone gave me a ride home, but when I got there, I couldn't stay. I walked to a motel and spent the night there. I cried for hours before eventually falling asleep. That night I had the most unusual dream that I will never forget. I was in a coffee shop with a man that I thought was Peter. Somehow though he was different in a way that I couldn't understand. I stayed in the motel for a few more days, and on the third day when I woke up in the morning the man from the dream was standing there. I was still too drowned in sorrow to care; I was actually comforted because he reminded me so much of Peter. I remember asking for his name hoping he would say Peter but instead he said Twenty."

"Twenty?"

Twenty laughed taking in my expression. "Yes."

"Are you gay?"

"No," he said.

"Then why?"

Kemlek turned to me. "Twenty found me like he found you and Raina."

"So some man shows up that looks like your dead husband, and you just decide to come here?"

"Well, there was a bit more discussion before I left the remnants of my old life behind."

"Why would you choose this?"

"Nicole, do you believe in fate?"

"I don't really know."

"I did at the time, and I still do. I believe Twenty came to me for a reason. Perhaps it was Peter's way of telling me to move on. Death was his; this was mine. Our love, as brilliant as it was, was gone. So Twenty gave me the opportunity to come to his land, a place where things were different. But to come here, I could no longer be a human. I was given a chance to become a Mecrathin, which is a very difficult process. The transformation spells are performed by a special council, and the pain they inflict isn't just for a few hours. It goes on for three entire days. You are given many chances to stop, but somehow I managed to make it through. I am now what is called a Death Mecrathin, which is really just a Mecrathin that was once human. In the end, the pain was worth it."

"How did you stand coming here?"

"I had my new home, and I had Twenty. He certainly made the transition easier."

Raina smiled. "That's remarkable. I always wished I could have been born a human. The world sounds so exciting."

I could tell what she was doing. Her smile was perfectly conservative and her words had an unusual eloquence to them. She knew very well I thought Kemlek's story was insane.

I cast my eyes to the ground, and when I glanced back up I could tell by the way Twenty was watching me he had been reading my thoughts. He didn't say anything though. Instead he smiled rather lightly and asked, "Well, who cares for a drink?"

"Oh, yes," Raina said her smile now relaxed.

"Definitely," Kemlek nodded in agreement.

Just like that a shadow figure appeared with a tray of vodka. The vodka had been poured into glasses, but Twenty didn't bother with that. He just took the bottle and pushed it to his lips. "Now that is nice, Nicole."

I thought I might as well try some, so I took the bottle and took a very, very small sip. "Oh my God." I coughed. It was absolutely awful. It didn't even have a taste. It just burned like liquid fire.

"Well, you don't like it."

"No," I said handing him back the bottle, which he made vanish. A pleased smile splayed across his face.

"I'm surprised. The cyanide usually adds quite a kick."

"Cyanide? Are you trying to kill us?"

"Oh, don't worry. It won't harm you. You're immortal now."

Kemlek turned to Twenty. "Maybe she will like the other drinks."

I barely had time to wonder what he had planned before I heard a faint hiss and Raina's shriek. "Not more snakes," she groaned.

I, on the other hand, was ecstatic. A snake cake was one thing, but actual real live snakes was a whole new scale of wonderful. I recognized the species immediately.

The first was a black mamba which, despite its name, wasn't actually black. Its very long body was a dark grey, and the inside of its mouth was black. The second snake appeared much larger than the mamba with its light grey body and expanded hood that beheld a beautiful spectacle pattern, an Indian cobra. While both the mamba and cobra were very interesting, they paled in comparison to the last snake: a beautiful gaboon viper with a large triangular head, greatly narrowed neck, and a series of pale sub-rectangular blotches running down its back interspaced with dark yellow edged hourglass marking. It seemed to gaze right through us.

I stepped back a little to truly take in the beautiful creatures with the power to kill, gracefully resting upon the shoulders of barely visible Shadow Figures.

"Would you like to try their venom?" Twenty's voice startled me so greatly I practically jumped out of my skin.

"Excuse me?"

"It won't harm you. Poison is as good as alcohol."

"You do know a bite from a gaboon viper will cause you to bleed out from every orifice in your body."

His sadistic smile crept onto his face. "Exciting."

"No, it isn't."

Kemlek laughed. "She certainly doesn't trust you."

"No, I don't trust him, and I don't know why I should. Do you know what it's like to be so inferior to someone that you will never be able to fight back? You're not even a victim. You have no idea what it's like to be owned by someone."

He was smart enough not to reply to the statement.

I thought Twenty may have been upset with me for what I had just said, but his gaze actually softened. "Emotions are running high today. I assure you, though, on the breath of my life this venom will not harm you. In fact, you may find the perfect poison to subdue your pain." He held the tray out to me, the glasses upon it shimmering like forbidden gems.

After a few hesitant moments, I did try them. The cobra venom tasted like spices, and I could feel hot air blowing all around me. I could hear the music people played to hypnotize cobras. I felt like I had been hypnotized and trapped. It was as if someone had wrapped me in a heavy blanket and then pushed me into a cage. The feeling was somewhat warm, but the warmth turned to heat that rose into my lungs and threatened to suffocate me.

Next was the mamba's venom, which tasted bitter and immediately ripped away the blanketed and caged feeling. Where there was once warmth, there was now a frigid chill. Forget subduing my pain. This was bringing the memories back in bucketfuls. I felt myself falling, and it was if I were standing at the bottom of a very deep well trapped and scared while someone poured freezing water over me. Emotional and physical pain attacked with vicious talons.

I felt as if I were Goldilocks searching for the right porridge. The first was too hot, the second too cold; would I find salvation in the third? The glass of gaboon viper's venom had just passed my lips when the sweetness overwhelmed me. Oh, how delicious it was—better than sugar cubes or flat ginger ale. In all of my life, I had never tasted anything like it, and the pleasure, the beautiful feeling of blissful happiness, like dancing in the sunshine surrounded by all of life's wonders.

"Oh," I sighed. "That one was wonderful. Raina, you should try some."

"No, no thank you."

"What do you have against snakes? They are wonderful creatures."

"The first night I was here Twenty made the whole floor just crawl with snakes."

"Did you really?"

"Oh, yes, it was rather amusing. She screamed as if her bones were being torn from their sockets."

She shuddered. "It was horrible. I wouldn't even speak to him for a week."

"I should do that again. It was very nice."

"You are mean." She was struggling to remain serious, but in the end, that failed, and we all ended up laughing.

From there the mood continued to lighten. We ordered more drinks: gaboon viper venom for me, vodka for Kemlek and Twenty, and a nice white wine for Raina. The conversation was friendly. Kemlek had a lot of good stories to tell, plus there was talk of the future. Visiting Mary, an extravagant Paris honeymoon. Twenty said maybe we could even visit my children. At some point, Kemlek pulled out one of those pocket calendars and helped us plot dates.

I hadn't been this happy in a long time, but as the hours went on and the other guests began to leave I felt very worn. My head was aching, and my throat was becoming increasingly sore. The room was spinning slightly, and my stomach felt as if someone has taken it and flipped it upside down.

"I don't feel well. Could I get a chair?" I whispered, my voice lit with a note of hysteria.

Twenty turned his attention to me abruptly as if I had suddenly just caught on fire. "Are you all right?"

I went to shake my head no, but suddenly the floor rose up beneath me, and I collapsed. It felt like seconds later when I opened my eyes and remembered thinking how comfortable cobblestones were, but I wasn't lying on the floor. I was in a bed, a soft white comforter tucked over me, and fluffy pillows underneath my tired, aching head. This wasn't my bed or my room.

From just looking around it would appear that I was alone, but I knew Twenty was almost certainly nearby. "What happened?"

That was all it took, and there he was. "You're awake."

"What happened?" I repeated.

"You fainted. You've been out for about an hour."

"Great. A whole hour of my life wasted." I pushed the covers aside and went to sit up, but as my feet touched the floor, the dizziness overwhelmed me.

"I don't think that's a good idea." He tucked the covers back over me. "Why don't you just rest for now?"

"I can't. You don't understand. This is my wedding night. I'll be ruining it for Raina too."

"Calm down. She told me she would wait for you."

I put my head back and sighed in defeat. Just as I was thinking that maybe I was starting to feel a bit better, a sensation of pain overtook me, vicious knives tore my throat to shreds from within. I always thought to have a sore throat was horrible; this was beyond that. This pain was indescribable. "Help me," I barely managed to choke.

"Side effects," he murmured, and then he vanished.

I wanted to scream at him for leaving me, but sprouting wings and flying might have been an easier feat to accomplish. My muscles began to spasm, and my body trembled. I was locked within my suffering, the magic key hidden from sight.

Twenty returned just as I thought I could bear no more. He handed me a heavy crystal glass that my shaky hands barely managed to hold onto. "Drink this. It will make you feel better."

I put the cup to my lips, but the smell was sickening. I looked back at him, and his expression was actually so frightening I forced myself to swallow a little. It had the metallic taste of blood. As it began to increase I realized that it may not have been the drink. Blood was actually dripping from my mouth. "Oh, what did you do to me?" Just as the words left my mouth I realized I was talking and the pain was gone.

"Feel better?"

"Why did it hurt so much?"

"Blood had built up in your throat. Now you finish that and I'll be back."

I didn't want to leave, but he was gone before I could make a formal protest. Without much choice I slowly drank down the vile concoction sip by sip. With each swallow, the blood flowing from my mouth increased until I finished and the blood stopped altogether. At least I wasn't in pain anymore although my dress was soaked in red. Besides not being in pain I was also extremely lucid and tired.

The crystal glass was so heavy, even fully emptied, I lost my grip and watched it fall anticipating the sharp noise of it shattering beyond repair. Inches from the ground it froze suspended in mid-air before vanishing.

"Good old magic." Twenty came to my bedside and continued to work. His wonders made blood disappear. "How are you feeling?"

"Weak."

"That's the medicine. Just relax. Your suffering will be over soon."

"Am I dying?"

"No, my dear."

"For argument's sake, say I was. Tell me something."

"And what would that something be?"

"Why am I here, and please don't say because I'm female, pure and delicate, or you wanted my soul. Why out of all the people you could have chosen did you choose me?"

He laughed, and his face took on a distant look. "Okay, a long time ago I couldn't stand living the existence life had given me. The cards were being dealt but not in my favour. The man I called my guardian, whom I had loved and thought of as a father, tried to kill me. He pushed this horrible knife to my throat and told me I could start acting like a Mecrathin or rot in Haven. I left that night, and I was, as you would call it, homeless. I didn't really know what to do. I came across this land that no one wanted and claimed it as my own. I built this castle using the magic I had practised all of my life. You think using magic is easy? It took me many months to build this, and I nearly killed myself during the process. So then I had this beautiful castle, and soon after I helped Kemlek. Life seemed to make a little bit more sense. I was ready to find a victim: a fair maiden to be mine. I found Raina. First I didn't particularly want her, but she was on a slexing list, and for some reason, I found the idea of her dying unbearable. Now that I had her I continued my search. There was this book that Mecrathins would look through to find Shadow Figures, Bloodens and, best of all, mortals. I knew I wanted a human, but all the girls were bland, living lives that scarcely belonged to them, basically just conforming to what society wanted them to be. Then there was you. You knew exactly who you were, and you weren't trying to be anyone else. I claimed you right away so when I wanted in a few years you would already be here.

When you were about sixteen, I wanted to take you, but you had a path marked by mortals. I settled for the fact that I was allowed to emerge into your life and test how you responded to fear. As I watched you and waited for fate to play out, I found that someone else had claimed you, my dear cousin Meraish. The council, which establishes our basic law in the Shadow Lands, said let the mortal's path run its course and settle our dispute ourselves. As I was dealing with this, an old rivalry had come forth. You see, when I took this land it was not exactly mine to take. This had belonged to Xephius, and as his revenge, he took Raina from me. I would have taken Raina back right away, but at the time I had you to worry about. What Meraish and I had to wait for was the chapter of your life with Kyle to resolve. Until then we were struggling to maintain our claim by keeping you very afraid. When you were in Paris, it was free game for both of us. You were on the flight home when I managed to trap Meraish in a realm of chaos that took him a long while to get out of. After that, you know the rest. In the end, though, I had you and your companion. I've probably bored you enough with the details of my past."

"No, it's fascinating. I've always found you so intimidating. It's nice. You sound almost human."

The slightest smile crossed his face, but it was pained and somewhat sad. "You know I care about you."

"Yes," I replied hesitantly. "Is everything all right?"

"I have something unfortunate to tell you."

"What is it?"

He took a deep breath. "The day you asked Raina to marry you. Before you proposed how were you feeling?"

"I was sad. We'd had a fight, and I remember thinking that I wished my dad were here because he always helped me through things."

"The reason you felt such a strong emotional response is because at that moment your father died."

"What do you mean, he died?"

"He had gone back to Afghanistan. He and several other soldiers were on morning patrol when he stepped on a landmine. Two other young men died alongside him."

The first thing I thought was, who would read his obituary? He had always looked online and in local newspapers for reports of soldiers' deaths. He'd put them in his scrapbook so he would never forget. He told me since they had sacrificed their lives the least we could do was offer them a simple memory. Would anyone else remember him?

"How could he be dead?" I whispered barely believing it.

"I'm sorry, Nicole."

"No, he can't be dead." I was crying now, the tears pouring down my face like the raging waters of an unsettled river.

"This is why you're going home. Your mother and father will be very happy to see you."

This alarmed me. "Wait. What do you mean, going home? They are dead. Even you can't reverse death."

"Not your old home; you're going to a better place."

"No, you're killing me." I tried to get up, but he was, of course, faster than I was. He put his hand around my throat silencing my protests. "What are you doing?" He smiled, and my heart felt as if it had turned to ice. I had never been this scared. "What are you doing to me?"

"I have severed the spells that have bound you here, first with viper's venom and then with the drink you just finished."

My body began to feel unnaturally light. "What about Raina?"

"Just relax."

"No, what about Kemlek? He talked about fate. Why did you find me so interesting? Maybe because you were meant to? This all happened for a reason. I started to blink so rapidly I could barely see him. "Don't make me leave please." I was screaming as loud as I could struggling to hold onto to him. Just as I thought all of my efforts were futile, he seized my wrist and pulled me from the bed. The fading feeling stopped and kneeling upon the cobblestones I felt entirely whole.

"This is what you want."

"Yes."

He stood there as if he were contemplating this. I climbed to my feet with great difficulty, and when he spoke again, the usual sadistic edge had returned to his voice. He shoved me against the wall and sunk his fangs into my throat. Pain coursed through my blood like molten lava, and screams escaped from my mouth. As his fangs tore from my wound, he held tight to my arms so I wouldn't fall. We were pressed close against each other, and I could feel his heart beating rapidly. He placed his hand against the wound, and I let out a short breath as I felt it heal. "Raina will be happy to see you." He clasped my hand within his and pressed my fingers to his lips.

The next thing I knew I was in my room.

"Oh, Nicole, are you all right?"

Raina's voice was music to my ears as I wrapped my arms around her and kissed her full on the mouth. "I'm beyond all right. I have you, my love." She was as beautiful as ever wearing red pyjamas, her hair curly from the braids. "Oh, you look so comfortable."

"Oh, I know those dresses are so heavy."

She helped me free myself from the miles of thick white fabric and slip into comfortable black pyjamas. We were both so tired. The moment that our heads hit the pillows we were out. Everything was perfect: my wife beside me, our little animals asleep at our feet. I guess even Twenty fit into the happy perfection.

The most pleasant of subjects were woven into my dreams, and I slept soundly for several hours. In the middle of the night, I woke up clawing the skin on my left wrist, which burned furiously. I fumbled to turn on the lamp to see what was wrong. At first, I thought the black markings were clusters of spiders. Upon closer examination, I realized they were two words. Judging from the redness of my skin I understood that my decision had earned me my new tattoo which read:

Tortured Innocence

Acknowledgements.

Thank you to my amazing family and friends for supporting me while I was writing this book. These are the wonderful people who encouraged me to never give up, and to follow my dreams no matter what. There are too many people to name here. However, I would like to thank one of my best friends who was my first fan. That would be Shelbie Leclerc. You are awesome Shelbidore. Last, thank you so much to Sigrid Macdonald. You took my manuscript and polished off all of the rough and jagged edges. You are the best.